2041 22497

P9-CQA-630

DATE DUE

For more than forty years,
Yearling has been the leading name
in classic and award-winning literature
for young readers.

Yearling books feature children's
favorite authors and characters,
providing dynamic stories of adventure,
humor, history, mystery, and fantasy.

Trust Yearling paperbacks to entertain,
inspire, and promote the love of reading
in all children.

OTHER YEARLING BOOKS YOU WILL ENJOY

DONUTHEAD, *Sue Stauffacher*

CRASH, *Jerry Spinelli*

MUDVILLE, *Kurtis Scaletta*

TOBY WHEELER: EIGHTH-GRADE BENCHWARMER
Thatcher Heldring

THE PENDERWICKS, *Jeanne Birdsall*

HOOT, *Carl Hiaasen*

CORNELIA AND THE AUDACIOUS ESCAPADES OF
THE SOMERSET SISTERS, *Lesley M. M. Blume*

HOLES, *Louis Sachar*

TWO HOT DOGS WITH EVERYTHING, *Paul Haven*

The Girl Who Threw Butterflies

MICK COCHRANE

A YEARLING BOOK

McLean County Unit #5
204 Kingsley

Sale of this book without a front cover may be unauthorized. If the book is coverless, it may have been reported to the publisher as "unsold or destroyed" and neither the author nor the publisher may have received payment for it.

This is a work of fiction. Names, characters, places, and incidents either are the product of the author's imagination or are used fictitiously. Any resemblance to actual persons, living or dead, events, or locales is entirely coincidental.

Copyright © 2009 by Mick Cochrane

All rights reserved. Published in the United States by Yearling, an imprint of Random House Children's Books, a division of Random House, Inc., New York. Originally published in hardcover in the United States by Alfred A. Knopf, an imprint of Random House Children's Books, a division of Random House, Inc., New York, in 2009.

Yearling and the jumping horse design are registered trademarks of Random House, Inc.

Visit us on the Web! www.randomhouse.com/kids

Educators and librarians, for a variety of teaching tools, visit us at www.randomhouse.com/teachers

The Library of Congress has cataloged the hardcover edition of this work as follows:
Cochrane, Mick.
The girl who threw butterflies / Mick Cochrane.
p. cm.
Summary: Eighth-grader Molly's ability to throw a knuckleball earns her a spot on the baseball team, which not only helps her feel connected to her recently deceased father, who loved baseball, it helps her in other aspects of her life as well.
ISBN 978-0-375-85682-2 (trade) — ISBN 978-0-375-95682-9 (lib. bdg.) —
ISBN 978-0-375-89160-1 (e-book)
[1. Baseball—Fiction. 2. Pitchers (Baseball)—Fiction. 3. Sex role—Fiction. 4. Grief—Fiction. 5. Mothers and daughters—Fiction. 6. Friendship—Fiction. 7. Buffalo (N.Y.)—Fiction.] I. Title.
PZ7.C63972 Gir 2009
[Fic]—dc22
2008015986

ISBN 978-0-375-84610-6 (pbk.)

Printed in the United States of America

10 9 8 7 6 5

First Yearling Edition

Random House Children's Books supports the First Amendment and celebrates the right to read.

For my sister, Sue Cochrane

Acknowledgments

For support during the writing of this book, I am grateful to Canisius College. For certain facts and lore pertaining to the knuckleball, I am indebted to Ben McGrath's essay "Project Knuckleball," which appeared in the *New Yorker*. Thank you to those who read and commented on the manuscript: Ron and Marlys Ousky, Jack Williams, Mary Cochrane, Sue Cochrane, and Lon Otto. Special thanks to my wonderfully insightful editor, Erin Clarke, and to the amazing Jay Mandel and Charlotte Wasserstein. And heartfelt thanks, finally, always and all ways, to Mary, Sam, and Henry, the home team.

CONTENTS

In preagricultural societies, powerful butterfly
goddesses represented the closely linked forces of
death and regeneration in the world.
—Butterflies of the East Coast: An Observer's Guide,
Rick Cech and Guy Tudor

I discovered in nature the nonutilitarian delights that I
sought in art. Both were a form of magic, both were a game of
intricate enchantment and deception.
—Vladimir Nabokov, Nabokov's Butterflies

Throwing a knuckleball for a strike is like throwing a butterfly
with hiccups across the street into your neighbor's mailbox.
—Willie Stargell, Pittsburgh Pirates

1. A HEARTBREAKING DREAM ABOUT TOAST

*O*n Monday, after band rehearsal and intramurals, when Molly got home from school, her mother was sitting at the kitchen table going through the day's mail. It was after six, daylight saving time now, and still light, thank god. Even in Buffalo, the snowiest, grayest place on earth, spring eventually came.

Her mother had changed from her work clothes into her white designer sweats, matching pants and top with padded shoulders, which made her look to Molly like a fencer—all she needed was a little red heart.

She had cable news playing low on the countertop portable, a bottle of water and a pile of catalogs in front of her. It was what her mother did after work. Her ritual unwinding. She'd page through the glossy daily stack of catalogs one by one, turning the pages mechanically, looking irritated, angry even, fierce lines on her forehead. It seemed mysterious to Molly. Was her mother mad at Eddie Bauer? At Pottery Barn and Talbots? Dissatisfied with L.L.Bean's selection of boots and raingear, with Williams-Sonoma's pots and pans? It didn't make any sense. Her mother occasionally bought stuff, blouses and sweaters usually, always the same color, teal, which was weird enough—how much teal-colored clothing do you need, really?

As far as Molly could tell, her mother almost always returned whatever she bought. The UPS guy brought packages, and her mother opened them, unpinned and unfolded and held things up, sometimes tried them on. But then she'd usually just reassemble the packages and readdress them. She drove them around in her car for a few days and eventually dropped them off at the post office. To Molly, it seemed like a lot of work. Why subject yourself to such misery? What was the point?

Molly had learned not to interrupt her. Her mother was in some distant, ticked-off, unreachable place—the Planet of Inexplicable Exasperation. Molly put down her backpack and saxophone case, grabbed an apple from the fridge, sat down, and waited. There was nothing that looked like dinner happening anywhere in the kitchen. *Why bother cooking for just the two of us?* her mother had gotten into the habit of asking. Sometimes, with her dad at work, they used to make dinner together, Molly and her mother. They used to wash and chop vegetables and talk and even joke a little.

Molly liked it—it was like their own little cooking show. But no more, not for a long time. That show got canceled. Nowadays they mostly ordered out, subs or Chinese, pizza and wings. Molly missed her dad's cooking. He had only a handful of meals, spaghetti and stir-fry and omelets and meat loaf, that was his rotation, nothing fancy, but always tasty.

On television the square-headed security czar seemed to be changing the threat level while baseball scores crawled across the bottom of the screen. The Cubs had beaten the Pirates, 12–1, which pleased Molly, because it would have pleased her father. They were his team. He'd grown up listening to their games on the radio. The Cubs were lovable losers. They hadn't won the World Series for something like a hundred years. No matter. Her dad had always paid attention to the scores, and now, out of habit, Molly couldn't help but do the same.

"So how was your day?" her mother asked, her eyes still scanning the Sharper Image catalog in front of her—ionizing air cleaners, massage chairs, turbo-groomers.

"Fine," Molly said. Most days this was the right answer. It meant that she had negotiated another day without disaster, steered her little boat through the rocky waters of eighth grade without capsizing. She hadn't failed anything, she hadn't been given detention. In the past ten hours she'd done nothing to ruffle her mother's sense of well-being.

"What about rehearsal?" her mother asked. Sometimes she wanted more. What her English teacher called "supporting detail." She needed to "show" not "tell" her mother about the fineness of her day. Specifics. Molly would offer up something, a success, a little academic triumph she'd been saving—"You know that social studies test I was studying for? I got a ninety-eight!"

This was just what her mother wanted: evidence that Molly was a Good Kid on the Right Path, a girl making Smart Choices, the daughter of a Good Mother. Yes, her father had died six months ago—*exactly* six months ago; today was the anniversary, the fourth of April. But she was doing fine, she was resilient. Molly understood her part in this story perfectly: She was the brave-hearted poster girl, Miss Difficulty Overcome.

"We're playing a movie medley for the pops concert," Molly said. "*Star Wars, The Pink Panther.* I might get a solo."

"That's great," her mother said.

"And I lent Ryan Vogel my last reed. I need to get some more."

"That was nice of you."

What Molly didn't tell her mother was that Ryan, the other tenor player, who had toxic BO and dog breath, who was a volcano of rude eruptions and nasty remarks, had pointed toward her case with his own last, wrecked, saliva-covered reed and grunted something—she'd recognized only "gimme." She'd tossed him her entire pack and hoped he'd leave her alone. There was nothing nice about the transaction; it felt like a holdup, a mugging.

"Very nice of me," Molly said, and smiled a dopey, mock-charming smile. She framed her face with her fingers and tilted her head. "I'm a very nice person."

There was so much she couldn't tell her mother. How, for example, she had dreamed about her father again the night before. It was nothing especially dreamlike, nothing weird or unusual, nothing symbolic. On the contrary, it was beautifully ordinary. Her dad, sitting across from her at the kitchen table, spreading jam on a piece of toast, wearing his favorite plaid shirt, frayed at the collar, his weekend shirt.

In the dream her dad smiled, a little sadly, maybe, as if he knew something she didn't, and handed her a plate with the toast on it, two slices, strawberry jam, cut diagonally, and it looked perfect, the most delicious thing imaginable. She could smell that warm-toast smell, even in her dream, the best, coziest smell in the world. And when she was wrenched out of her dream and back into the world—her mother rapping on her bedroom door as she walked by, "Six-thirty, Molly, time to get up"—it was terrible, like another death, just as cruel.

What would be the point? Maybe her mother had her own dreams. In the past six months, Molly had come to understand that the most important stuff, what was closest to the bone, was just what you never talked about. There were no words for it. A heartbreaking dream about toast. The trivial and silly is what you spend your day chattering about. You could ask your friends how they liked your hair, but you could never ask them what you really wanted to know: Is there hope for me, yes or no?

"So this week is softball tryouts, right?" her mother said. "Wednesday. You ready?"

"I don't know."

"What do you mean, 'I don't know'?"

Her mother didn't really like sports. She didn't play anything herself—she sometimes went to a gym, but that was work, not play—and she didn't watch. On Sundays during football season, when everyone in Buffalo was glued to their televisions watching the Bills, her mother liked to go grocery shopping. And then talk about it: how deserted the store was, how the chip and the soda aisles looked as if they'd been ransacked. It seemed like a kind of bragging, an announcement of her moral superiority. She was above professional football.

Baseball belonged to Molly and her dad. When they used to watch a game together, her mother rarely joined them, not even for the World Series. She'd pull some work papers from her briefcase or start on some slightly disagreeable household chore. "You two enjoy yourselves," she'd say, and then go off to not enjoy herself.

"I'm thinking I might not play this year," Molly said.

"But you love to play ball!"

Her mother never seemed to get it. What she and her father watched on television was baseball. Not softball. When they used to play catch in the backyard, it was with a baseball, not a softball. She was not a tomboy, just a girl who liked baseball. To Molly, a softball just didn't feel right. It was too big to grip properly. It was too light, weirdly insubstantial. Softballs reminded her of the oversized, mushy balls they used in elementary gym class, "kittenballs," their teacher called them.

She'd played softball last year, was something of a star because she could hit and catch and throw hard. They put her at third base because she had a good arm, a strong overhand throw—she couldn't get the hang of a softball pitcher's peculiar underhand delivery—and was able to fire it across the diamond to first with something on it. They won some of their games. She had some friends on the team: Tess Warren, who played shortstop, a very good athlete, and funny, too—she could imitate most of their teachers and sometimes would shout encouragement to teammates from the bench in their voices—and Ruth Schwab, their red-headed pitcher, a lefty, whom Molly called "Ace."

But her most vivid memory of the season was from late in their last game. They were in the field. There was a girl in left field moving in some odd rhythm. It was Lucinda Baxter. First one foot came forward, then the other. She was leaning forward intently, her arms swinging rhythmically at her sides. Finally, Molly realized what was going on: The left fielder was tap-dancing! Molly was at third, working her gum, thinking about guarding the line late in the game, and her teammate was practicing a dance routine.

She didn't really dislike softball; she just wasn't all that interested. There was something second-class about it, for sure: people said "girls' softball," but nobody said "men's baseball." The roundhouse windup, the kneepads, the cheers and chants from the bench, like playground jump-rope songs. It seemed, well, a little girlish, fine if that was the sort of thing you went in for. But it didn't have much to do with the game she and her dad watched—the distances and proportions were off, the uniforms and dress not quite right, everything a few degrees off. It was like baseball translated into some foreign language.

Molly almost felt bad about it, her preference for baseball, as if she might be guilty of being insufficiently committed to the idea of girl power, Mia Hamm, gender equality, and all that. Which had nothing to do with it. She just happened to like baseball better, that's all.

But to her mother, baseball, softball—it was all the same, a senselessly complicated game with balls and bats. "It would be good for you," her mother said. "Fresh air, exercise, time with your friends, all that."

Her mother wanted Molly involved in after-school activities so Molly would be accounted for until after the workday was done. Her mother wanted her constantly busy, active, achieving. Maybe she believed that if Molly's schedule was sufficiently jammed, there would be no time to be sad.

So then, this is where it started: Molly said out loud what she was thinking. Normally, she'd keep it to herself. She'd arrange her face appropriately, say the right nice things, and find some subversive way to do what she wanted. She might "forget" the day of softball tryouts, say, discover a sudden pressing need for extra after-school help in math that particular day. She knew very well how to get her way, quietly. She could be a good-girl guerrilla.

But not this time. It wasn't a decision, really; it was some kind of accident. Like dropping something, like tripping. Her lips betrayed her.

"It would be good for *you*," Molly told her mother.

Now, suddenly, Molly had her mother's undivided attention. She looked up from her catalog. Now she was all ears. "What?" she said. "What did you say?"

"What works for you—that's what we're talking about, aren't we?" Molly said. Her voice didn't sound nice. "*Your* schedule, what makes *you* happy. It doesn't matter what *I* want."

"I see," her mother said. This was mother-composed, mother-above-it-all, businesslike mother. During the day, she did things on the telephone, in meetings, at the computer. She worked for a bank but never touched money. She solved problems for customers, except that her customers weren't real people, not the folks you see lined up waiting for the next available teller. They were corporate clients, never an old lady with a social security check to cash, not a kid with a pile of first-communion or graduation checks. They were businesses in other states, more people in offices who did things on the telephone, in meetings, at the computer. Now she was going to solve Molly.

"Are you concerned about your schoolwork, too much homework?"

"No."

"Is it the competition? Are you worried about making the team? Do you not like the coaches?"

"You haven't got a clue, Mom," Molly said.

"So give me a clue. Tell me why you don't want to play," she said. "Explain it to me."

"I don't want to," Molly said. "Because I don't want to." Her mother looked pained. "What am I supposed to do—make you a spread sheet, put my reasons in a PowerPoint presentation? If I made you a pie chart, would you leave me alone?"

"You played last year and you loved it," her mother said.

"How would you know?" Molly was cooked now, she knew that. She'd passed the point of no return. "Did you come to any of my games? Do you even know what position I played?"

It didn't get any better after that. Molly said some things

she knew she would regret but, feeling inflamed, in the altered state of anger, she said them anyway. Her mother lost her executive cool pretty quickly after that. She used the word "ungrateful" and the phrase "the thanks I get." This signaled that the discussion was over; there would be no more back-and-forth. What would follow was a monologue and then, most likely, tears.

Her mother looked angry and tired, her body tight with tension. She looked like she needed to spend some time in one of those massage chairs she'd been studying in the catalog, a lot of time. Molly felt sorry for her. She had a tough job and a not-so-nice daughter, and on top of that, now she was a single parent. It wasn't what she'd signed up for either. But Molly felt sorry for herself, too.

Molly stood up. Enough. Later, they would make up, apologize, agree to forget all about it, promise to do better next time. Molly knew what to say to make it happen. But not now. She didn't feel up to it. Now she just wanted to be alone.

2. SOME SERIOUS JUNK

*I*n the garage Molly found the baseball gear stowed under the lawn sprinkler and garden hose in a big plastic trunk. She lifted the top—it was a little like a treasure chest—and there were baseballs, softballs, three bats, batting gloves, a rubber home plate and a set of bases, her glove, and her dad's. Now, for the first time, his glove seemed like something from the distant past, an earlier era, another life. It looked sad and lifeless.

It was a big floppy piece of worn leather, a Wilson A2000 model, the best ever, he used to say, which had been, believe it or not, a wedding present from Molly's mother. Her dad told the story again and again. Molly never minded;

she liked to hear it again and again. She liked thinking about her parents as young and romantic. They met in an English class at a college in Wisconsin; they fell in love and got married right after graduation. He gave her a fancy watch, and she, knowing that he was crazy about baseball, a hardcore fan since he was a little kid, gave him a glove. Molly could imagine the exchange: her dad with his little jewel box, her mother with a big box, their mutual delight. He'd never had a nice glove, and she wanted him to have the best. It was huge. It didn't catch balls; it swallowed them whole. It was a big leather Venus flytrap.

Molly felt afraid to touch it. It didn't seem like one of his possessions—it seemed like him.

She grabbed her own beat-up glove and slipped it on. Now, when her whole life didn't seem to fit right—like a new pair of shoes that pinched, everything too tight or too loose, a blister forming—now her well-worn baseball glove was a small comfort. Over the years it had been molded to the shape of her hand. It was as soft and familiar and accepting as a teddy bear. It was one thing that fit perfectly.

She'd had her own first tiny glove when she was a toddler. At some point her father must have taught her a pitcher's windup. She'd seen her little self perform it on a family video. Out in the front yard, their shutters a dark blue then, which she couldn't remember, on a bright summer afternoon that she couldn't recall either, there she was, wearing pigtails and a Cubs cap and a T-shirt, toeing an imaginary rubber, pumping her arms, rocking and pivoting and then miming a big overhand pitch toward the camera. Even at that age she didn't really throw like a girl. She had excellent mechanics.

Molly knew that other girls had tea parties with their dads. She played catch with hers. It wasn't weird, it wasn't cool, it was just what they did together. She never thought much about it one way or another. She took it for granted.

They used to go into the backyard and throw the ball back and forth. It was like one never-ending game, with breaks. They played catch when Molly was in elementary school, they played catch the summer before her dad's accident. As the years passed, they stood a little farther apart, and Molly threw the ball harder, but it was the same game.

Molly loved the rhythm of it, throw and catch, throw and catch, the gentle pop of the ball in her dad's glove, a little puff of dust. It was comforting, calming, almost hypnotic, like meditation maybe. If she wanted to tell her dad something, she liked to tell him while they were throwing the ball back and forth. Good news, bad news, some scrap of a story from her day. It came out, unfolded itself naturally while each of them would throw and catch, throw and catch. Much of the time, though, they were silent. They were connected and content, the ball passed back and forth between them, and there was no need to speak.

Molly used to like to pitch to her dad. She polished her toddler's windup summer after summer in the backyard. She'd pitch entire imaginary games. He'd announce the batter and call out balls and strikes. It was a goofy, meaningless game, but Molly enjoyed it.

It required attention, for one thing. She needed to focus on her dad's big glove, her target, imagine the ball going right where she directed it. It was hard work that felt good. Throwing in the backyard to her dad on a hot summer day was the one time she wasn't embarrassed about sweating.

Some big league pitchers grunted when they threw hard, and sometimes so did Molly. And there was some drama in their games, too—a 3-2 pitch with the bases loaded in a tied game. But just for fun, with nothing really at stake. None of those hollering, overexcited, red-faced parents and coaches. Afterward, win or lose, it didn't matter, they'd sit on the deck and drink pop.

Her dad flashed her signals. One finger meant fastball. Two fingers was a curveball, which Molly couldn't really throw and her dad wouldn't permit at her age—"you'll hurt your arm"—so she just pretended. Three fingers was a changeup, an unexpected slow one. Four fingers was a special pitch, their secret weapon. The knuckleball.

Molly grabbed a scuffed baseball from the bottom of the trunk, tossed it into her glove, and walked out into the backyard. It was dark now, a few scrappy clouds being blown across a silvery quarter moon. Her mother had flipped on the back floodlight, a small gesture of reconciliation maybe.

Molly could see her mother in the kitchen, still sitting at the table, hunched over the mail. The image of her reminded Molly of the paintings of Edward Hopper, one of the American artists she and her classmates were supposed to be learning to appreciate. If it were a painting, something in a gallery, it would be entitled *Tense Woman Reading*. A study in isolation. Molly didn't really want to add to her mother's anxiety or raise her blood pressure; she didn't want to be another gray hair. It gave her no pleasure to complicate her mother's life. She was willing to be a go-along when she could. But the prospect of another season of softball, of having to watch Lu Baxter tap-dance her way through another inning—she couldn't take it.

Next door, she could see the Rybaks sitting around their dining room table, Mr. and Mrs., little Caitlin in her booster seat, Kyle dressed in his white karate outfit. Technically, they were in a suburb, but only three blocks outside the city limits, it didn't feel like a suburb. There were trees and sidewalks and some old people. There were no cul-de-sacs; the garages weren't attached. The houses were close together. Molly had a clear view of the Rybaks' dinner.

It wasn't nice, but Molly was jealous of their perfect little family unit. There seemed to be three or four big serving dishes on their table, and Molly wondered what was inside them. She was tired of takeout.

Molly walked over to her spot, where she stood when she played catch with her dad. The lawn was scraggly still and brown, but at night, under the lights, it looked fine. She looked across the yard to where her dad used to position himself. She tried to imagine him there, putting down a sign.

Once Molly had asked him, "Do you think a girl could ever play in the big leagues?"

She was still pretty little. She'd only recently figured out that of all the players they watched on television, not one was a girl. Her dad paused and thought about it. Even when she was small, he never talked down to her, he didn't offer up the chirpy, cheerful lies most parents handed out to their kids like Kleenex ("Of course you can, honey! You can do anything you want to!"). If she asked him a question, he answered it, for better or worse.

"Well," he said. He tugged at his ear and thought about it. "I don't think she could be a position player. Not a power hitter. Muscle mass and all that—sorry."

Then his eyes lit up. Molly could practically see the

15

lightbulb above his head. "But sure," he said. "A girl could play in the big leagues. A smart girl. It's possible. It's definitely possible. A pitcher. She'd have to have some serious junk. A trick pitch."

"Like?" she asked.

"Like a knuckleball," he said. "The old butterfly ball."

To throw a knuckler, you gripped it with your fingertips, your nails really, kept your wrist stiff, and let go of it as gently as possible. If you did it right, the ball didn't spin at all. You could see the laces, practically count them. It really fluttered—like a butterfly.

The first time her dad threw her his knuckleball, she couldn't believe it. How do you make a ball not spin? How do you make it wiggle like that? It was like a magic trick. Right then and there, Molly wanted to know how it was done.

Her dad showed her—some old coach had shown him, years ago—and she practiced. Eventually, she mastered it. She was no more than nine or ten at the time. In their backyard games, Molly threw it more and more. Her dad would sometimes complain because a knuckleball could be hard to catch. It was completely unpredictable. It would drop at the last minute, bounce, and hit him in the shins. Even though he'd gripe, Molly could tell he was proud of her.

Her ability to throw a knuckleball was an amazing talent, completely without interest to just about anybody else in the world. If she'd been double-jointed, or capable of belching the alphabet or turning her eyelids inside out, that would have been different. Something like that would've knocked 'em dead at the lunch table or at sleepovers. If she'd been a phenomenal speller, she might have ended up on television. But a knuckleball?

Still, it made her happy. It felt great to be so good at something. When she was in the backyard pitching to her dad, and the floater was working—darting and dipping, her dad whistling in admiration—all was right with the world. It didn't matter if she'd bombed a quiz that day, didn't matter if her mom was frazzled and angry, didn't matter if her chin was weird and she had giraffe legs, didn't matter if the world was full of terrorists. At that moment, when she was winding up and letting it go, everything was okay. She felt intensely present, alive.

The knuckleball wasn't just a pitch. It was an attitude toward life; it was a way of being in the world. It was a philosophy. "You don't aim a butterfly," her father used to say. "You release it." Each pitch had a life of its own. It wasn't about control, it wasn't about muscle. Each floating and fluttering pitch was a little miracle. It was all about surprise. To her, though she would never say so, every knuckleball she threw seemed like a living thing, each of them full of impish high spirits.

Molly assumed her pitcher's stance, leaned in to get the sign. Four fingers was the old butterfly ball. She took a deep breath. She started her windup: took a little step back and pivoted. This was a kind of dance, too, Molly understood. She lifted her front leg and found her balance point. She drew her arm back, pushed off, stepped forward, and let loose.

Maybe because it was her first pitch of the year, maybe because it was nighttime, maybe the moon was working some magic, maybe something else, but for whatever reason, this one was special. The ball seemed to dart from her hand, as if it was eager to take flight. In the light, she could see its perfect nonspin, the laces vivid and clear. If there had been a message written on the ball, she could have read it. The ball wobbled and wiggled, dipped and darted. Before it landed in a flower bed and rolled under a bush, it would have crossed the plate knee high, diabolically unhittable, and into her dad's big glove.

"Pretty pitch, Mol," he would say. "That was a beaut."

Suddenly it hit Molly, an idea with the electric force of inspiration, an idea so beautifully right, so perfectly obvious, it seemed inevitable. A perfect strike. Of course.

3. HER STUPID PLAN

"**Y**ou're gonna do what?" Celia whispered, too loud, and Mr. Zelmani gave them a look. It was second period. They were in Honors English, supposedly revising their *Great Expectations* essays.

They'd been friends forever, Molly and Celia. Molly couldn't do anything crazy without telling Celia. They'd met on the bus the first day of kindergarten. Celia had a little beaded frog dangling from her knapsack that first day, and Molly admired it. Next day, she handed one to Molly. They'd been best friends ever since.

"I'm going out for the baseball team," Molly said.

"Not softball?" Celia said.

"Baseball," Molly said.

"Not girls' baseball?" Celia asked. "Not intramurals? Baseball-baseball?"

Celia was not big into sports, but even she understood it meant something to play on the boys' baseball team. There was real status in being on the team: Not everybody who tried out made it. They played regulation baseball—a full-sized diamond and all that—and competed against schools from all over the area.

"Baseball-baseball," Molly said. "The real deal."

By this time Mr. Zelmani was busying himself with Lonnie House, a sweet kid whose expectations, Molly feared, were not that great. Mr. Zelmani was kneeling beside Lonnie's desk, trying to read what he'd written. Lonnie was smart as could be, brilliant maybe, the class artist, but his work was always late, incomplete, crumpled, smeared.

"You're not kidding," Celia said. "You're serious about this."

In October Mr. Zelmani and the English class had sent Molly and her mother a big flowery card with an ornate message of condolence and everyone's signature. A few of her friends had shown up at the wake, filed grimly through the line, and offered limp handshakes and tentative hugs. A few more were at the church for the funeral. Back then Molly and her mother had turned into grieving robots, nodding mechanically, hearing the same words again and again, saying the same words again and again.

Of all her friends only Celia had stayed until the end, only Celia had come to Molly's house and eaten sympathy cake and potato salad with her, had let her cry and had never spoken a single supposedly consoling cliché. And when Molly came back to school, only Celia hadn't seemed frightened of her.

"It's a tryout is all," Molly said. "I'm going to try."

"Any other girls trying out?" Celia asked. "Any other girls *ever* try out?"

"I don't think so," Molly said.

Celia grinned. She'd always had a rebellious streak. When the school's dress code had been revised the year before to exclude clothing with slogans, Celia had shown up wearing a T-shirt with the words FREE SPEECH printed across the back. From her older brother Michael, who was some kind of alternative vegan activist, she'd picked up some radical politics. If asked, she was prepared to argue that the omnipresent Nike swoosh was in fact also a slogan, advocating exploitation of third-world labor and all that. She had a whole spiel she was prepared to deliver. But no one asked; no one objected. Probably they knew Celia would be too much to handle.

She was not shy, that was for sure. She was part of the horn section in band with Molly. She played the tuba. All her parts were boring, of course—it wasn't like she was ever going to play a solo. But Molly always figured that her friend simply relished the chance to make a big noise.

"This is big news," Celia said. "You're breaking new ground. You're a pioneer. That's what you are."

"If you say so," Molly said.

"Really," Celia said. "I mean it. You're like one of the pioneers we read about during Women's History Month. You're Amelia Earhart."

"Oh, shut up," Molly said.

Celia stiffened suddenly, and Molly knew Mr. Zelmani must be standing behind her. He was a big man, but he walked softly, on little cat feet.

"Joe is crucial to the novel because he offers Pip unconditional love," Celia announced. "Wouldn't you agree?"

"Oh yes," Molly said. "Absolutely."

Mr. Zelmani managed to make a little sound in his throat, a kind of muffled cough that somehow expressed perfectly how not-fooled he was. But Molly knew he wouldn't yell at her. Six months later, he was still cutting her slack.

At lunch Celia quizzed her about her plan. The only thing Celia didn't ask was why. For that Molly was grateful. She didn't think she could justify or explain herself, convince anyone that this made sense. It just felt right, and maybe Celia, bless her, understood that.

"What does your mom think about this?" she wanted to know.

Because Celia had three brothers and two sisters, and because Molly had none, they'd always been fascinated with each other's lives and families, curious.

"What's it like to be a lonely child?" Celia had asked her back in first grade. Molly had corrected her—"it's *only* child"—but she'd never forgotten Celia's phrase.

Until Celia asked, Molly had never thought of herself as a lonely child. But it was true, she was. Sometimes. Compared to her best friend, she was. Celia didn't have to go out for a sport—her family was a team. The last of the big families, like some sort of sitcom. There were eight people, six

22

or seven of them living at home, one bathroom, two cars. Every morning was a fire drill, every day of the week was like a field trip. When Celia wanted some peace and quiet, when she wanted to hear herself think, she came to Molly's house.

When Molly wanted to lose herself, she went to Celia's. There was always something going on. A pack of boys shooting baskets in the driveway. Somebody standing at the stove in sweats scrambling eggs. Her dad reading the paper at the kitchen table and holding forth to anyone who'd listen about the state of the world. There was always music in the house, too—somebody blowing a horn or banging on their scarred upright, the Beatles blasting out of somebody's bedroom.

Molly liked the happy noise. She envied the fact that Celia's parents didn't—couldn't—pay so much hawkeyed attention to her, her every grade, her every mood, what a certain look or remark *meant*.

"I may not have mentioned it to my mom," Molly said.

"It may have slipped your mind," Celia said. She laughed and offered Molly half of her pita and hummus. Somehow, Celia's mom, an intensive-care pediatric nurse, got all her kids' custom-made lunches right. Molly's mom gave her money to buy, but the choices were almost all gross. So usually she just bought a drink, maybe some pretzels, and then leeched off Celia and pocketed the change.

"What about the coach?" Celia wanted to know. "Who is it?"

"Mr. Morales," Molly said. He was a tall, bland-looking guy she'd seen doing lunchroom duty. He taught social studies.

"Is he a misogynist?" Celia asked. "Does he hate women?"

"I know what it means," Molly said. "I don't think so." A couple of weeks before, as she'd come toward him to toss the remains of her lunch in the trash, Morales had looked her in the eye and smiled. *Am I supposed to know you?* Molly wondered. Then it occurred to Molly that he was just one human being acknowledging another, wishing her well, offering her a little bit of unearned kindness—not the sort of thing that happened all that often in the school cafeteria. He looked amused, as if he and Molly were sharing a wordless joke, both knowing what a funny thing it is to be in a cafeteria on a Tuesday afternoon.

"He seems pretty mild," Molly said. "I don't think he hates anybody."

Celia pulled a pear from her lunch. With a plastic knife she sliced off a big, juicy-looking piece and slid it across the table to Molly.

"You know who thinks this is great?" Celia asked. "You know who couldn't be happier?"

"I know," Molly said.

At the end of the school day Celia came by Molly's locker. "Are you ready?" she wanted to know.

"As I'll ever be," Molly said. She'd just been thinking that if she hadn't stupidly announced her stupid plan, she'd be able to slink home now, forget all about it. Softball didn't seem so bad, hanging out with Tess and Ruth. But she'd coughed it up and Celia knew, and now she had to go through with it.

"What are you gonna wear?" Celia asked. "Something dramatic, I hope. Something that makes a statement."

24

"A statement," Molly said.

"That's right," Celia said. "You want to wear something that says, 'I'm all woman, but I am going to strike your butt out.' That look."

"Funny you should say that," Molly said. "That's exactly what I had in mind. Cleats and tube socks, sweats and T-shirt, hoodie."

"Perfect," Celia said. "Especially the hood. It adds mystery. Who am I underneath? Who am I really?"

This was fun. Molly loved Celia's goofy riffs and hated to cut her off. She would have loved to linger. But she had to get moving. She lifted her bag from the bottom of her locker. In half an hour she was supposed to be on the practice field.

"Here," Celia said. "Take this."

She put something into Molly's hand. It was a small clear stone, like an ice chip.

"It's beryl," Celia said. "Or maybe bauxite. Or maybe something else. I'm not sure. But it's definitely a mineral that starts with a B. And it's definitely lucky."

"You stole it," Molly said. She knew Celia had a study hall in the earth science classroom.

Celia wrapped Molly's fingers around the stone, the way your grandmother gives you money for ice cream, making a tight little package for safety, giving her hand a squeeze.

"For luck," Celia said. "Put it in your shoe, hide it in your glove."

4. WELCOME TO BASEBALL

*F*or the first half hour, all they did was stretch. Arranged in a huge circle around Coach Morales, Molly and nearly thirty boys slowly and systematically worked the muscles in their shoulders, backs, arms, and legs. They rotated their necks, spun circles with their arms, rolled their wrists, yanked their elbows above their heads, twisted their trunks; they got down, extended their legs, and tugged at their toes.

Morales positioned himself in the center of the circle and exercised right along with them. In school he seemed slightly geeky, a tall guy with thinning hair, dressed in a yellow short-sleeved shirt and striped tie. He seemed awkward patrolling the cafeteria. But on the field, in sweats, with a ball cap on his head, sunglasses perched on the brim, he looked lithe and supple. He moved like an athlete, like a ballplayer. Here, he looked so much more natural than he did in the cafeteria, so much more at ease. This was apparently his element, his real home turf.

Morales gave instructions and counted off repetitions. His voice was insistent but patient, calmly demanding they contort and twist their limbs beyond any reasonable limit. He sounded like a drill instructor who'd studied Zen, or maybe hypnotism, like one of those perky TV fitness gurus but heavily tranquilized.

Molly was self-conscious at first. She could just imagine how foolish she looked. But before too long, she lost herself in the sheer physical effort involved. She could feel the muscles in her back and upper arms, muscles she seldom used, and the sting wasn't completely unpleasant. It reminded her that she had muscles. She felt like she was getting acquainted with the complex machinery of her own body, all her moving parts.

Molly had arrived on the field just a few minutes before Morales had blown his whistle and, without any formal welcome or introduction, started them off stretching. There'd been a big group of boys gathered around the third-base bench. She recognized most of them. Ryan Vogel, the BO king, her saxophone partner, was there. Lloyd Coleman, Mario Coppola, Grady Johnston. They were boys she knew by reputation to be the jocks, the alpha males. In school they wore sports jerseys and expensive sneakers, ate lunch together, all members of the same exclusive club. Next year, when they moved on to high school, they'd become the varsity lettermen; they'd take cheerleaders to homecoming. They lived at the top of the food chain.

They were chewing gum and spitting sunflower seeds, pushing and pawing each other and kicking up dirt, knocking off each other's caps. They were tall as men, some of them, had ropey muscles in their arms, but they still acted like little boys. The whole scene at the bench looked a lot like fourth-grade recess.

She had lingered behind the backstop, maybe ten yards away, and pretended to adjust her cleats. She untied and retied each a couple of times. Then somebody must have noticed her, because the hubbub suddenly ceased. Molly was afraid to look up. She tied her right shoe one more time, as slowly and as deliberately as she could. There was the sound of some whispering. Then Morales had blown his whistle.

Before long, Molly heard some grumbling from around the circle. "What is this?" someone to her left said. "Yoga?"

"If I wanted to do ballet," someone else muttered, "I would have worn my tutu."

The trouble with boys and sports, it seemed to Molly, was that it was all about them. The good ones figured they already knew it all; they just knew they were headed to the varsity and then the big leagues. All their lives they'd been told how wonderful they were. She'd watched them on the playground, the hotdog, hothead stars, cheered by their doting dads. They'd been told they could do no wrong. If they struck out, it was the umpire's fault. If they lost, it was because somebody else blew it.

For them, it wasn't about the team, and it wasn't about

the game. It was as if baseball existed just so they could be good at it, so they could show off. They really weren't all that different from the dance girls who lived for the sparkling outfits: *Look at me, look at me*. Molly wondered if these boys really loved baseball, the sound and smell of it, the rhythm of it, the leather and wood, the grass and dirt, the story and surprise in a good game.

Morales put them in lines to do some running, but not the usual sprints. First they ran lifting their knees as high as they could, which you can't do fast. Then he asked them to skip—skip! There was practically a mutiny right then and there among the boys. "This is stupid." "I'm not skipping." But they all did, or at least tried.

Molly took an early turn and remembered the carefree joy of skipping, the happy exuberance of it. It made her remember what it felt like to be five years old. She jogged back to her place in line and watched the others take their turns. The sight of a tough guy like Lloyd Coleman trying to skip, and doing it badly, all the while looking over his shoulder to see who might be watching—it was delicious. On videotape it would have been blackmail quality. It was something Molly wanted to remember so she could tell Celia about it the next day at lunch. It would be good for some laughs.

After everyone took a few turns skipping, they ran backward, and then sideways, crossing one leg over the other. It was hard not to get tangled up, but Molly concentrated, and by her second time through the line, she'd gotten the hang of it.

Finally, Morales called them in and told them to take a

knee. Molly was breathing hard now but seemed no more winded than any of the boys. A couple of them were wheezing pretty radically. They sounded like two-pack-a-day men.

"Okay," Morales said. "Welcome to baseball."

He told them that in the next week, they would get to know each other.

He wanted to see what they could do. He hoped to teach them some things.

His voice was so soft, Molly had to lean forward in order to catch what he was saying. In Molly's experience, gym teachers and coaches were holler guys, human bullhorns. But not Morales.

"Baseball is all about doing little things right," he said. "That's what we're going to work on." Molly liked the way he talked. Calm and thoughtful. She liked his message, too. She wanted to believe that little things could make a big difference. It was corny, but when Morales said it, it sounded true.

"So let's begin at the beginning," he said. He produced a baseball from his back pocket. The boy next to Molly groaned. What followed was a brief introductory lesson on the art of throw and catch: grip, angle of the arm, release point, spin, lots of attention to footwork.

It felt oddly like being in school, but Molly, who was a good student, didn't mind. She was near the front and enjoyed watching Morales's slow-motion demonstrations. He was a kind of baseball mime, moving with a smooth, practiced authority she couldn't help but envy.

Molly found herself trying to remember all of this, to find words for it, so that she could turn it into a story. It was what she did. She'd give Celia the story about Lloyd Coleman trying to skip. But this story, Morales and his baseball, which he produced from his pocket like a magician pulling a rabbit from his hat or a silk scarf from his sleeve, this one, Molly realized, would have been for her dad. She would have told him in the backyard as they tossed a ball back and forth. Celia wouldn't get it. Her mom wouldn't care. Now this story would stay untold. It would be a tree that falls in the forest, unheard.

"All right," Morales said. "Grab a ball and find a partner."

This was the moment she'd been dreading. Up to now it had been okay for the boys just to treat her as invisible, to act as if she really weren't there. She'd been expecting abuse and resistance and instead simply got ignored. The boys apparently didn't know what to say to her, so they hadn't said anything. Maybe back in T-ball or peewee soccer they'd had a girl teammate, but not since then. They didn't know what to make of her, perhaps, so they just didn't see her. It was fine by Molly—it made things easy. Invisible wasn't all that bad.

But now she needed a partner. How do you find a partner if you're invisible? She'd survived the buddy-up traumas of elementary-school field trips, mainly thanks to Celia. She'd endured the humiliations involved in sixth-grade boy-girl dance instruction, watching the boys edging away from her and jockeying for turns with the glamour girls. But this was worse. All of a sudden, as if on some secret signal, every boy on the field seemed matched up. They were pointing at each other, nodding, moving off quickly to assume positions across from one another. Only Molly seemed to be standing in place. Everyone else was moving away from her, fast. It was like some playground game, and she was obviously "it." Here, she was some kind of leper, a baseball untouchable.

She considered her options. She could just stand there, like a pathetic dork, until maybe Morales told her what to do. Or she could, she could—what? She tried to think.

Just then she felt a tap on her arm. It was Lonnie House, the boy from her English class. Molly hadn't seen him on the field, or maybe hadn't recognized him. He was wearing a dusty Buffalo Bisons cap at a peculiar angle, his hair sticking out from beneath it in unexpected places.

"Molly," he said. "Play catch?"

"Play catch," she said. It was a little miracle. She felt like kissing Lonnie, her unlikely savior. But she didn't give anything away. "Sure," she said.

They positioned themselves across from each other and waited for Morales's instruction. Molly felt a great surge of emotion, relief and gratitude. This disheveled boy had *seen* her, he had spoken her name.

While they were playing catch, Morales moved down the line with a clipboard, asking for names and positions.

"Molly Williams," she said—and then pulled a low throw from Lonnie out of the grass on one hop. He had a funny sidearm delivery. He was fast but wild.

"Nice scoop," Morales said. "Where do you wanna play?"

"Pitcher," she said.

"Okay," Morales said. He made a note on his board and moved on down the line.

Molly liked that he didn't seem especially shocked, or outraged or excited, or even all that interested in the fact that on a team of Gradys and Lloyds, Matthews and Zachs, she was sure to be the one and only Molly. To him, apparently, she wasn't a girl, she was a ballplayer.

Near the very end of practice, while the infielders and outfielders threw each other grounders and fly balls, Morales asked the pitchers and catchers to join him on the mound.

Mostly it was the thoroughbreds, Lloyd and Grady and Desmond Davis, the boy stars. Lonnie came along, too, and stood next to Molly, while Morales described a good delivery. "It's all about balance," he said.

"I'm a catcher," Lonnie said, half to himself, half to Molly. Though he didn't seem like the type. Catchers were the squatters, guys named Pudge, with gnarly hands, who barked like bulldogs at their teammates. Was Lonnie telling Molly or trying to convince himself? Molly hoped he wasn't following her around because he felt sorry for her. But it occurred to Molly that maybe he needed a buddy, too.

Time was short, but Morales wanted to see them pitch. He paired them up, each pitcher with a catcher, Molly with Lonnie—the two of them already like some kind of couple. Grady Johnston was first and threw a rocket. But Morales didn't like his release point, or what he was doing with his left arm, and told him so, while Grady looked decidedly displeased.

A couple of other boys threw, and then at last it was Molly's turn. She started her windup, and her motion felt perfect, smooth and sure. She knew how to do this. Except this time the ball didn't do what it was supposed to do. It did not travel on a line into her partner's mitt. It sailed over his head. Way over his head. Like into outer space. Molly just stared. It was spectacular and horrifying, like a car accident.

There was some snickering from down the line. "That's what I'm talking about," somebody said.

While Lonnie was chasing down her wild pitch and the boys were hooting it up, Molly could have made her exit. Turned then and there and walked off the field. "Cut your losses" was an expression her mother sometimes used, and this was Molly's opportunity to do just that.

No one would have blamed her. Her softball friends would have welcomed her back. But she didn't do it. Maybe just because she couldn't imagine telling Celia about it without using the word "quit." She could feel her friend's lucky stone, or mineral, or whatever it was, tucked in her left sock. She made herself look attentive as Morales, who seemed oblivious to where the pitch actually went, praised her mechanics, her rock-solid balance.

Her dad had an expression that he sometimes used, too. "Gut check." When a pitcher was in a jam, when things looked bad, the bases loaded, say, nobody out, late in the game, when the pressure was on, that was a gut check. It's the moment you find out what somebody is made of.

So she'd launched her first pitch into the stratosphere. It was embarrassing. Big deal. Lloyd Coleman could laugh himself silly. Molly had had worse moments, much worse. These guys had no idea. This was nothing.

5. GEOGRAPHY LESSON

*M*olly had gone to bed early that night in October. In order to have time to shower before school in the morning, to eat some breakfast and catch the bus, she had to be up and moving by six-thirty. That night, though, she'd set her alarm for five-thirty, so she'd also have time to study. There was going to be a map quiz in social studies, and she wanted to have one more look at her notes.

She had always liked geography, had always liked maps. She loved her dad's old-fashioned light-up globe. When she was a little girl, she'd give it a spin, close her eyes, and point, and where her finger landed, that was a place she was going to visit someday: Fiji, Cameroon, the Marshall Islands. She loved saying the names of faraway places. Her dad, who could be Mr. Let's-Look-It-Up, had a huge Rand McNally atlas on his desk that he would consult with the least provocation.

Molly liked the irregular shapes of the land masses. She could stare at them the way some people did at clouds, the crazy puzzle pieces of the continents, every map an abstract work of art. But as she tested herself on the Mediterranean, she kept confusing the Ionian and Aegean seas, the islands of Crete and Cyprus. She was always muzzy-headed at night, at her best early in the day. With a few minutes of study in the morning, Molly was confident she'd nail it. Acing a quiz, getting an A, earning good grades like merit badges—back then, it had seemed so important. Back then, if she'd blown a test, that was a bad day. If she'd made a stupid calculation in math, if she'd accidentally skipped an essay question in English, that would be a tragedy. What did she know about tragedy?

When she flicked off her bedside lamp that night, Molly could have drawn a perfectly accurate map of her own world. Her mother was downstairs in the family room, half watching something on television, looking through some work papers. She'd stay up for the news—she made fun of the local anchors but watched anyway. She'd maybe watch a little bit of *Nightline*, then come up to bed.

Her dad was downtown, working the graveyard shift at the newspaper. He was in the big newsroom she'd visited many times over the years, perched on the chair she used to spin and roll around in, staring into his computer screen, a framed picture of her next to his cup of pencils.

He'd always wanted to be a sportswriter. His heroes were those old-time, cigar-sucking, typewriter-pounding fellows.

Guys named Red and Lefty. At the college where he'd met Molly's mother, he'd studied journalism and even had his own column in the school newspaper. Molly knew this because she'd discovered copies of it stashed in the attic: There was a grainy photo of her young dad and his byline.

But somehow he ended up on the copydesk of the *Buffalo News*, where he didn't actually write much of anything except headlines and captions, the sentences under pictures that hardly anybody even read. *Kimberly Royce of West Seneca enjoys a sunny afternoon in Delaware Park with her four-legged friend. Will McMaster of Cheektowaga bows his head in prayer Sunday during the opening of Kingdom Bound.* He cut out extra words and fixed other people's mistakes, put commas in all the right places, made sure that everyone's name was spelled correctly and that the names of federal agencies were appropriately capitalized. He used to joke about irate local bowlers calling him to complain if he misspelled one of their names in the weekly scores. But he rarely talked about what he did at work anymore. When asked, he made a backhand gesture, a bored, wordless dismissal.

Molly sometimes wondered if his work, all the repetition and all the attention he was forced to pay to such trivial things, made him sad. She worried that his job was taking the starch out of him. He seemed grayer lately, slumped. It occurred to Molly that her father needed some kind of project to cheer him up, something he could throw himself into. He'd never been much of a tool guy; he didn't do birdhouses. She decided that he ought to write a book. It was something she intended to mention to him, but she hadn't gotten around to it. She was waiting for the right moment.

Molly was beat; she fell asleep right away. Sometime

during the night she heard something, or rather, later, she remembered hearing things, half hearing, really. Some kind of minor commotion downstairs. Voices, the telephone, the doorbell? It seemed remotely dramatic, urgent but distant and muted, like a television show from another room.

At five-thirty her alarm buzzed. Molly tapped it and got right up. Her mom was a big fan of the snooze alarm, but it didn't work for Molly. She hated the feeling of bobbing along half asleep, getting buzzed every five minutes. If you have to get up, get up—that was her theory. She went through her morning routine—shower, hair drying, getting dressed, making her bed—crisply and quickly. What had she been thinking about? It was hard to remember, it seemed so long ago. It was another lifetime. Was she thinking about Mediterranean islands? Was she worrying about her grades? Hoping that her friends would notice her new sweater?

She had grabbed her backpack and headed downstairs. Her mother was in the kitchen, sitting at the table with Mrs. Rybak. Mrs. Rybak?

Her mother looked as Molly had never seen her before. She'd been crying; her eyes were red. She had a crumpled tissue clutched in her hand. But beyond that she seemed utterly different. Transformed. She looked almost bruised and raw somehow, as if she'd been beaten. She looked as if she'd been peeled.

"Sit down, Molly," her mother said.

Suddenly, at that moment, the geography of her own little world shifted. Something fixed and vast, a continent, had in an instant disappeared. An ocean dried up. Suddenly she had become an island.

6. IT COMES FROM A COCOON

"**S**o did you wow 'em?" Celia wanted to know. "Did you make an impression?"

They were at the lunch table, working their way through a stack of crackers, Celia tossing them across the table to her one at a time, like a blackjack dealer. They were nutty-tasting, stone-ground, multigrain wafery things, a little scary-looking but good. But Molly felt like she should tease her friend anyway.

"How about some normal food once in a while?" Molly asked. "How about a normal cracker? Something a little more in the mainstream. Not so left-of-the-dial. I mean, what have you got against Ritz?"

But Celia blew her off. "They're Swedish," she said, as if that explained everything.

"An impression?" Molly said. "I would say, yes, I definitely made an impression." Molly told her about her space launch of a pitch at the end of practice.

"Big deal," Celia said. "One pitch. It doesn't mean a thing."

"I guess not," Molly said. When Celia said it, it sounded true, irrefutably, self-evidently true. *One pitch doesn't mean a thing.* Of course. It sounded like something from a book, like something Ben Franklin might have said.

Molly told her about all the stretching—she was sore as could be—and the boys' muttering gripes about it. She told her how Lonnie House had stepped up to play catch with her—Celia raised an eyebrow, about to say something, but Molly kept going. She told her about Lloyd Coleman trying to skip.

"I love it," Celia said. "Your coach should make him do Pilates. Wouldn't that be hilarious?" From her lunch bag she produced a block of suspiciously pale, ripe-smelling cheese and started slicing off hunks with a plastic knife. She offered Molly a piece.

Molly just looked at it.

"Don't ask," Celia said. "Just eat it."

Molly spotted Mr. Morales patrolling the lunchroom in his yellow short-sleeved shirt. Now, to Molly, who'd seen him on the field the afternoon before, he seemed a little like Clark Kent or Peter Parker. It was as if he had once again assumed his everyday identity, knotted his tie again and become boring and mild-mannered. But Molly knew what she knew. There was more to Mr. Morales than met the eye.

40

He strolled over to their table and smiled. "Molly Williams," he said. It was partly a greeting, but it almost sounded like some sort of announcement or introduction. Probably he was just testing himself, trying out her name.

"Hi," Molly said. Here, she didn't know what to call him, wasn't sure whether he was "coach" or "mister."

"You threw the ball well yesterday," he said.

"She's an awesome pitcher, you know," Celia said.

"I'm sure she is," Morales said.

"She's got a secret weapon," Celia said. "A mystery pitch."

"Is that so?" Morales asked. He looked mildly curious, amused.

"It is so," Celia said. She looked over her shoulder and leaned forward conspiratorially. "The mothball," she stage-whispered.

Molly had a mouthful of juice, and it was all she could do not to spew.

Morales looked puzzled.

"A knuckleball," Molly said. "The butterfly ball."

Morales had seemed to be sort of humoring Celia, but now he was definitely interested. "You throw a knuckler?"

"My dad taught me," Molly said.

Morales looked at her as if he were recalculating something, adding "throws knuckleball" into the equation of who she was. "This afternoon you can show it to me," he said. "Your secret weapon." And then he strolled away, a lunchroom cop back walking his beat.

"Mothball?" Molly said. "Mothball?"

"What's the big deal?" Celia said. "What's the difference?"

"Mothball?"

"It comes from a cocoon, it has wings, it floats—"

"You," Molly said. "You are so . . ."

"What?" Celia asked. "I am so what? Tell me. I can take it. I can handle the truth."

"You are so . . . Swedish."

At practice that afternoon Molly was once again invisible, almost. She timed her arrival carefully, got on the field exactly at three-thirty. By this time the boys were already tossing balls back and forth, and Morales, back in baseball mode, was on the diamond with a rake, along with another man, smoothing the dirt around second base.

Molly stood behind the backstop and stretched a little, twisted her trunk back and forth. It was gray and misty, the sky dark as dusk practically. But in Buffalo this was typical. In Buffalo, any day in April without snow was considered spring. Molly's mother used to take some perverse pleasure in pointing out that Seattle had fewer cloudy days than Buffalo. You can look it up, she used to tell Molly's dad during their regular half-playful, half-deadly serious debates: Buffalo stinks, yes or no. The great gray gloom, her mother called it, depression on a stick.

Morales called them all together briefly and introduced the new guy—Coach V, he called him—and said he'd be helping out when he could. He had an old, weathered, leathery-looking face and a mustache that truly was pencil thin. He had a toothpick in his mouth.

"Grandpa," somebody whispered.

Once again they did the long warm-up routine, stretching and hopping and skipping. Molly liked it, the tug and pull of it, even though it hurt, maybe because it hurt—she was that weird. She remembered hearing that to get stronger, you destroyed old muscle cells and made new. She liked to imagine that she might be reconfiguring herself from the inside, getting quietly, invisibly stronger.

When it was time to play catch, Lonnie House appeared, his beat-up Bisons hat still off-kilter, holding up a ball, a wordless invitation, which Molly accepted.

They started tossing it back and forth. Molly hoped that Lonnie didn't feel sorry for her. She didn't want to be the object of charity. She hoped he wasn't a Boy Scout or something using her for a good deed. He didn't seem like the type, but what did she know?

Lonnie was a little bit of a puzzle. He didn't fit into any easily identifiable group. He wasn't a jock or a nerd. He was smart, though—Molly knew that. He didn't raise his hand, but he always *knew*; he was one of those. He wasn't a punk or a Goth or a stoner. It was hard to get a handle on him. On a standardized test, he was answer E: none of the above.

The one thing everybody knew about Lonnie was that he loved to draw. And he was good. Last fall Ms. Jacoby, the art teacher, invited or permitted him—Molly didn't know whose idea it was—to paint a mural on her classroom wall. What he produced was pretty amazing. It was a green landscape, a kind of dense rain forest, with a canopy, all kinds of fantastical animals half-hidden in the dark foliage, bush baby eyes peering out of the shrubbery, mole-ish creatures snuffling along the jungle floor, bright macaws perched in the branches, hummingbirds hovering. To Molly, it felt humid; she could almost hear the twitter and caw, the soft breathing. It wasn't real, but still, it was a place Molly would like to visit. It was like one of the places on the other side of her dad's globe; it was like her idea of Fiji.

Molly was thinking about Lonnie's rain forest, feeling her arm loosening up nicely, noticing that Lonnie's form was better today, he was coming over the top now, when all of a sudden she saw a look of alarm cross his face. "Molly, look out!" he hollered, and she thought, crazily, it was something from the sky, a bomb, a missile, some piece of debris.

A ball bounced up and hit her square in the shinbone. It rolled away, and Lloyd Coleman came over to pick it up. He had a nasty smile on his face.

"Sorry," he said, still smiling.

"Sure," Molly said. Her shin was killing her. She could feel a welt forming, but she didn't look. She wasn't about to give Lloyd that satisfaction. "No problem," she said.

"Better watch yourself," he said. There was something cold and hard in his face, something unfamiliar, something she couldn't immediately assign a name. But then it hit her, after Lloyd had turned and walked away, after she'd assured Lonnie she was fine, and she'd resumed throwing and catching with him. The word came to her, what it was called. It was hatred, that's what it was. Hatred, pure and simple. And it was directed at her.

Morales broke them into groups and set up various stations around the field. They charged grounders at one, fielded fly balls at another, practiced leading off and getting a quick jump at a third. Morales moved among the groups, a bat in his hand, which he sometimes used as a pointer, performing little demonstrations, making small corrections and adjustments in technique, keeping up a constant stream of encouraging patter. There were quick switches, balls flying, very little standing around, no time to chat. Molly did sneak a peek at her shin and found a nasty-looking knot about the size of a golf ball. She kept Lloyd Coleman on her radar. She raised her personal alert level to red. She didn't intend to get caught by another sneak attack.

Later Coach V threw batting practice. He had a short no-windup delivery: one quick step, and the ball came in straight and true, middle of the plate, half speed. He worked at a constant rate, regular as a metronome. Step and throw, step and throw, step and throw. Molly had never seen anything like it. He was a pitching machine with a mustache.

When it was Molly's turn, she stepped in and performed respectably. She had a short, compact swing from softball and usually made contact. She didn't try to kill it. She whiffed on the first pitch but connected on all the rest— sent two ground balls to the right side, a decent line drive over third base, and, on her final swing, a line drive up the middle. V gave her a little nod, a sign, Molly wanted to think, of approval.

Near the end of practice, Morales called Molly over to the right-field line, where he was working with pitchers and catchers. She jogged over, and he handed her a ball. "You loose?" he asked.

Molly nodded. The ball felt good in her hand. She stepped onto the pitcher's rubber positioned in the grass and looked in at the masked boy who was squatting behind a makeshift home plate. She couldn't tell who it was, not Lonnie, but whoever it was, he was set up solidly and giving her a good target.

"Let's see what you got," Morales said.

It was an audition, no doubt about it. What did she have? Molly had no idea, really. She took a deep breath and thought about throwing in her own backyard, all those games of catch with her dad, all those imaginary games. It was no different, really. The ball was the same.

She wound up and delivered a strike, which landed with a satisfying pop in the catcher's glove. The catcher, whoever it was, held it there for a moment. Was he surprised? Molly threw a few more pitches, not rockets by any means, but all of them in or near the strike zone with decent velocity. She felt good, smooth; she could do this.

"Okay," Morales said. "Show it to me." Molly looked at him. "You know," he said. "The floater. The mothball."

Molly couldn't help but smile. Celia's Swedish crackers and her big mouth. She gripped the ball with her fingertips, just the way her dad had taught her years ago, just as she always had. She wound up and let it go. Molly loved watching one of her knuckleballs in flight, but what she felt was not self-admiration at all, just simple curiosity. *What is this one going to do?* This ball started to come in high but then made a sudden swoop, a birdlike dive. It skittered past the catcher, who remained fixed in his squat, looking a little stunned. He got up and chased it then, and Molly glanced at Morales. He'd turned toward the infield diamond, where Coach V was still throwing BP.

"V!" he hollered. "Over here. Come have a look at this."

While Molly's catcher chased down the ball and returned it to her, Coach V ambled over and positioned himself next to Morales, both of them with their arms folded identically across their chests, waiting for her.

Molly felt beyond nervous now. "In the zone" is how she'd heard professional athletes describe that feeling of being right, in synch, and that's how she felt. She gripped the ball, reared back, and let another knuckler go, this one coming in waist high and at the very end making a hop, a little aerial hiccup, just enough to throw the catcher off— the ball glanced off the side of his glove and bounced off his kneecap.

The catcher took his mask off, and Molly saw that it was Ryan Vogel, her saxophone partner. He was shaking his head and seemed to be talking to himself, making some unhappy noise, gesturing accusingly in her general direction.

Coach V had a big crooked smile on his face. "Well," the old man said. "Well, well, well."

7. HARDBALL

*I*t was almost nine o'clock. Molly was sitting with her mother in the family room. It was an addition to the house, built when Molly was maybe five or six. She still remembered it vividly as her dad's big project. She could recall him studying the plans for what seemed like months, and once the work had actually begun, Molly remembered how every day he inspected what had been accomplished. Together they looked at beams and drywall. He took photographs. Molly loved the smell of lumber. Though not a handyman at all, her dad did some painting and last-minute finishing. It was just a room, carpeting and a couch and television, a sliding patio door and a fuel-efficient fireplace, but he was so proud of it. To her father, it wasn't just a room, it was an idea. He would never spell it out, but Molly understood that the idea involved bowls of popcorn and cups of hot chocolate, lounging on the couch, the Sunday newspaper. It was a place where you could wear pajamas and not worry about spills. It was where they decorated the Christmas tree and hung their stockings. It was where they watched sappy movies and baseball games together.

His own father, Molly gathered from bits and pieces over the years, was the man who wasn't there, a briefcase and martini and newspaper. He had died when her dad was in high school. He never talked about him. There were no warm stories. Molly somehow understood that his father was the man her dad didn't want to be. The family room must have contained his own idea of fatherhood.

The family room. That's what they'd always called it, but now Molly thought of it in quotation marks, the "family room." So-called family room. The two of them, Molly and her mother, didn't seem to constitute much of a family these days. Two people at Celia's would be considered an empty house, nobody home. Two people—if they were a club, they wouldn't have a quorum. If they were a team, they'd have to forfeit.

Molly's mother had established a position on the couch. She was a woman who needed gear—equipment, accessories—in order to watch television. Herbal tea, magazines and catalogs, daily planner, hand lotion. Not to mention her purse, in size and shape exactly resembling a horse's feedbag, that big, that deep, virtually bottomless, from which she might extract almost anything: lip balm, reading glasses, cell phone, restaurant leftovers, office supplies—paper clips, Post-its, a mini-stapler, you name it.

They were watching—not watching, that sounded way too focused—they were *absorbing* a cable news program, angry middle-aged men in red power ties hollering at each other from studios in different cities. One guy was making dire predictions about dirty bombs and subway smallpox, smiling a little bit with self-satisfaction, looking pretty pleased that terrorism was so good for his career. Molly was looking over her science notes, and her mother was writing something in her planner, but they were taking it in, both of them, secondhand current-events anxiety. Molly thought about making a comment to her mother, attempting a joke: What are the ill effects of twenty-four-hour cable news? Hasn't it been shown to cause nausea in laboratory animals? They used to laugh together sometimes about all the junk on television, the scandals and hypes, the stupid graphics, the snarly hosts. But there was something about her mother's demeanor. She had that do-not-disturb look. Molly let it pass, the urge to banter. She decided not to bother.

Her mother was right there in front of her, and still, somehow, Molly missed her. It didn't make sense, but it was true. She missed her mother who laughed, her mother for whom life was not one tedious task after another. It was as if that woman had been kidnapped—she might be tied up in a basement somewhere. And in her place there was this mother, a joyless impostor wearing her real mom's clothes.

Her mother was busy now sorting through a big pile of what looked like store receipts, yellow and pink duplicate something-or-others. Her stuff was spread out all over the place. It filled the couch; it spilled into little satellite piles next to her on the floor. If her dad had been present, Molly wondered, where would he even sit?

It had always been her mother's nature, Molly believed, to expand—to get bigger, louder, bolder, to fill up more shelves, spread out, invade new territory. Her father's personality was just the opposite. Under pressure he contracted, hunkered down, shrank back, grew silent. Because of that, to some kind of neutral observer—the woman who came once a month to clean, say—he wouldn't have seemed all that present. You couldn't miss her mother's stuff, acres of clothes and miles of shoes, her file-folder and magazine mountains, all the decorative doodads—wood carvings, wire-sculpture thingies, baskets and vases, ceramics, framed prints—that came and went and moved around constantly, and that Molly, taking her cue from her dad, never commented on and certainly never complained about.

Her mother even smelled big: When she walked through a room, her scent lingered long afterward. Evidence of her father's existence had always been real but more subtle. You'd have to know what you were looking for to spot the signs of him. A folded newspaper, pencil, and completed crossword puzzle. His keys hanging on a hook by the back door. A couple of cans of Coke in the back of the fridge.

And now, after just six months, Molly was afraid that little by little, bit by bit, the last traces of him were in danger of disappearing altogether. Some of her father's effects— that's what they call your stuff after you die—were gone now. They'd disappeared from the house. Molly had looked for them. She knew where they belonged, where they'd always been. She knew every nook and cranny in the house, where her mother hid presents. Molly searched on the top shelves and in the low drawers, behind the furnace. Things had gone missing. His golf clubs with their tassel covers. The grass-stained sneakers he wore when he mowed the lawn. Molly knew that her mother was responsible, but she never caught her in the act. Never saw her packing a box or dragging a bag to the curb, never saw her with tears in her eyes.

So it was a gradual, invisible, but profound disappearance, like erosion. The surface of the earth being transformed. But this was worse, really—it was intentional. It was thievery. Her mother was, if not a suspect, then what the police would call "a person of interest." In this case, the only one.

Molly stood and stretched. Her hamstrings were tender, and there was a soreness in her shoulders. Morales and his stretching. But it was okay. She liked the idea that she might be getting stronger, more limber.

Molly wandered into the kitchen and drew herself a glass of water from the tap. She looked back in on her mother—crossing something off one of her to-do lists from the looks of it, still achieving at this hour—and headed upstairs.

At the top of the stairs she made a hard right into her parents' bedroom. It was neat in a generic sort of way, inspired, Molly assumed, by a magazine, some designer's idea of simple luxury, or luxurious simplicity. It cost a bundle to look Amish. The bed, dressers, and bedside tables were light wood and clean lines. On the bed there was an eggplant-colored quilt her mother had paid a fortune for in Pennsylvania.

On her dad's side of the bed there was no book, which was wrong. Back in October he'd been reading a fat biography of Lincoln, and Molly was curious how far he'd gotten, but it had disappeared. His little digital alarm clock was still there, but probably not for long. It seemed somehow not right to Molly that it was still keeping time, still clicking off the minutes.

Alone in her parents' bedroom Molly felt sneaky and weird, like a burglar or a sleepwalker. But she couldn't help herself. Now she felt drawn inexplicably to her dad's closet. She'd visited a couple of times before, when she had a moment alone in the house, just to think about him, to feel him maybe, to breathe him.

She stepped into the closet and inhaled. He was a flannel-shirt, cotton-sweater, and jeans guy. For her dad, every day basically was casual Friday.

When she was little, she used to make him take off anything made of wool, anything scratchy, so she could snuggle into his vast, warm softness. She used to slip into his big shoes and shlup around the house. He used to put a shapeless canvas hat on her head, some kind of fishing hat, his yard-work hat, and Molly would wear it happily, despite her mother's protests ("That thing is filthy!"), because her dad had told her that the hat possessed magic powers. While she wore that hat, he told her, "No harm can come to you." She loved to hear him say those words.

Her dad's favorite brown corduroy jacket was still hanging in the closet. He'd had it as long as she could remember.

If he needed to look semidressy, that's what he'd put on—for a band concert or an open house at school, for a Christmas party. Sometimes he wore it to work over jeans. Molly's mother bought him new jackets from time to time, preppie gold-buttoned blazers and tweed herringbones. He'd thank her, admire them and try them on, and then the next time he needed a jacket, he'd be wearing the brown corduroy.

Molly took it off the hanger and slipped it on. It was way too big, of course; she was swimming in it. But she pushed up the sleeves. It was probably a look that Celia could pull off. With the right attitude, baggy could be hip. If Celia wore it, it might become a fashion trend, the Next Big Thing. Molly knew that she looked exactly like a girl wearing her dad's sport coat. No matter. The lining was smooth, and Molly liked the sensation of being encased once again in her dad's bigness.

There was something stiff inside the jacket's breast pocket. Molly reached in and pulled it out—a reporter's notebook, spiral bound, tall and thin. There was a pencil jammed into the wire. Molly flipped it open, feeling a flutter of excitement. There might be something in it from her dad: a note, a message, directions, advice, a map, something, anything. She would have been glad to find a grocery list, minutes from a boring meeting, some doodles. Seeing his handwriting would be like hearing his voice. But no. Every page was blank.

Molly took the pencil, touched it to her tongue, and held it poised over the pad expectantly, the way reporters do, waiting for a quote. She stared into the rack of his shirts

204122697

and chinos. On television, reporters were fearless. They could intimidate people with questions. They threw them like knives. Reporters shouted out what was on their minds and then demanded follow-ups. They played hardball. That was the name of the game.

Mr. Williams, I'd like to ask you about that night.

She'd been thinking about it for six months, and it still didn't make sense. He was not a reckless man. He was not like one of those drug- and booze-addled middle-aged rockers who wrapped a sports car around a tree every other month. He didn't drink. He signaled his turns and, as far as Molly knew, observed the speed limit. And yet, one night in October, driving the same highway he had many, many times before—hundreds, maybe thousands of times—he'd lost control, crashed through a guard rail and rolled down an embankment. Obviously Molly knew less than she thought she did.

If I may. With all due respect. There're some things we're still not clear about. Isn't it true, Mr. Williams, that again and again you were known to tell your daughter to "be careful"? Isn't it true that you would tell her this under the most ordinary circumstances? If she picked up a pair of scissors or sliced a bagel, if she was climbing a stepladder, getting on her bicycle, walking to school, lifting any object larger than a loaf of bread, isn't that what you would say? "Be careful"?

Molly could hear her mother moving around downstairs. It was a commercial break. Probably her tea was cold. Any minute she would notice Molly was gone and would investigate. Solitude was suspicious.

So let's cut to the chase. On that night in October, Mr.

McLean County Unit #5
204 Kingsley

Williams, when you drove home, as you had many, many nights before, with your wife and daughter at home—your daughter who needed you, Mr. Williams, who needs you—were you careful? Did you take care?

"Molly? Molly?" Her mother was at the bottom of the stairs, shouting up at her. "What are you doing up there? Are you all right?"

8. THE ART OF GRAFFITI

$\mathcal{T}$he next morning when Molly got to school, she found a message scrawled across her locker in black Magic Marker. GIVE IT UP, it said in thick letters, and after that the writer had added an ugly name, and then three exclamation points. As if one didn't do the job. Molly's first thought was of her dad, the copy editor. What would he think about punctuation in hateful graffiti? He'd taught her long ago that exclamation points, even one at a time, were usually excessive—no need to shout, he liked to say.

Her locker was near the end of a long corridor of science classrooms, a quiet neighborhood in the city of the school. Who besides her even knew it was her locker? *I know where you live*. That's what the stalkers always said to their victims in horror flicks. Next thing, they're hiding in your closet with an ice pick. These guys, her tormentors, they knew right where she lived.

So what am I supposed to do about this? Molly wondered. She had no experience in being a victim. She felt no desire to make a report, file a complaint. The last thing she wanted was to create an incident, get Vice Principal Niedermeyer on the case, be the subject of some sort of investigation. All she wanted, really, was to grab her English notebook and to go to class, get on with her day, business as usual. Now this.

It was still early, the halls nearly empty, but the bell was going to ring in just a few minutes. Molly found some tissues in her bag and tried to rub out the words but with no success. Leave it to these jerks to use permanent marker, she thought. She spit on the tissue and rubbed again, harder, but managed only to smudge the writing a little.

There was some light traffic in the hall, the clickety-clack of somebody's heels behind her, the squeak of sneakers. She kept rubbing, stupidly, uselessly.

She paused for a moment, and when she did, she sensed something. There was somebody standing behind her now, she could feel it.

"Losers," a familiar voice said. Molly turned. It was Lonnie House. He was kneeling, digging through his backpack. His hair looked as if it had been styled with an eggbeater.

"Hey," Molly said.

"Hey," Lonnie said. "Let me give you a hand."

"It won't come off," Molly said, but she just kept rubbing anyway, her tissue now a worthless, pathetic wad.

"You need some kind of solvent, like paint thinner," he said. "Something with alcohol."

He kept zipping and unzipping various pockets and compartments, pulling out pencils and brushes, a big eraser, tubes of what must have been paint, a small T-square, a drawing pad, more pencils.

"You really come equipped," Molly said. "You're an art store on wheels."

"I try," he said. "But right now, I'm coming up empty."

"Thanks anyway," Molly said.

"Wait a minute," Lonnie said. "That was just Plan A. There's also a Plan B."

He had a marker in his hand now, uncapped—Molly could smell it—and he was standing in front of her locker door, studying it.

"What are you doing?" Molly asked.

"A mural." Then, after just another moment of study, he went to work—filling in letters, darkening spaces, adding new lines and sweeping curves. The marker made little squeaking sounds, and Molly could hear Lonnie humming quietly under his breath. It was like he was some sort of art-making appliance, and what she was listening to was its motor. Or maybe with his pen in hand, Lonnie was a happy cat, purring.

Before long a crowd had gathered. Something unusual was going on, somebody was breaking the rules, and nobody was going to want to miss that. Not so dramatic as a fight, but still pretty good theater. Not bad for a Friday morning.

Lonnie meanwhile didn't even seem to notice that he had an audience. He just kept working, kept humming, his hand and arm in constant motion, making big sweeping lines, broad strokes. It was something to see him so assured, so bold. In class and on the practice field he sometimes seemed a little bit lost, but here he was the picture of confidence and focus. If he had been a ballplayer, the announcers would be saying that he was locked in—now he was in the zone.

When Lonnie finally took a step back to study his drawing, the hateful message was gone. It had not been erased or covered up—more like borrowed or stolen, transformed into something else entirely. In Lonnie's drawing, there were three long-limbed figures crowded together, like scarecrows, one hunched, one squatting, one standing upright. It took Molly a moment to realize it was a baseball scene: an umpire, catcher, and batter frozen at home plate, their eyes all fixed on a ball speeding toward them. The ball was trailing motion lines, which made it look fiery and dangerous, like an asteroid.

A few of the bystanders made some noises of surprise and admiration, and somebody started to clap, but all of a sudden there was an ominous silence. Molly turned her head and saw everyone scattering, walking away fast.

It was Niedermeyer, and he had something like a smile on his face. He was showing his teeth.

"My, my, my," the vice principal said. "What have we here?"

Molly found Celia in the library. Lonnie was nowhere to be seen. Was he being interrogated by Niedermeyer? It wasn't a pleasant image. Molly remembered how when Niedermeyer had led Lonnie away, he'd looked like someone under arrest—he'd looked handcuffed. But Lonnie looked a little proud, too, a little defiant, like a political prisoner.

They were supposed to be finding critical interpretations of *Great Expectations*, but actually Celia had been researching women in baseball. "You ever hear of Jackie Mitchell?" she wanted to know.

Celia pointed to a picture on the computer screen in front of her. In the photograph, a young woman in an old-time wool baseball uniform, a lefty, was following through after throwing a pitch. Somehow Molly knew that she wasn't just striking a pose, that she'd actually just delivered a pitch. Her eyes were following the flight of the ball, and she was biting her lip in concentration.

"Nope." Molly shrugged. "Never heard of her."

"Of course not," Celia said. "She signed a contract to pitch for the Chattanooga Lookouts in the 1930s. This was a professional team, a *men's* team, not that All-American Girls thing with Madonna and Geena Davis. She struck out Babe Ruth in an exhibition game. Even I know Babe Ruth. What do you think of that? Babe Ruth!" She looked at Molly, waiting for a reaction.

"Babe Ruth," Molly said.

"And then you know what happened?" Celia asked. "I'll tell you what happened. The commissioner of baseball, the great Judge Kenesaw Mountain Landis, gave her the boot. Voided her contract. Because baseball was 'too strenuous for a woman.' What a load of crap."

Finally, Celia noticed that Molly wasn't right and asked what was the matter. Molly gave her all the details. She told her about the hateful message, about all the exclamation points. She told her about Lonnie's Magic Marker mural, how Niedermeyer had busted him and let her off scot-free.

"Lonnie?" Celia asked. "Lonnie House? He came along and drew a picture over the message?"

"You should see it," Molly said. "It's really something."

"Lonnie is really something," Celia said. She smiled, a little wickedly.

It felt good to be talking to Celia. But telling Celia about what had happened made it feel more real, like something that had happened to her. What she understood, what she felt now, was that it was aimed at *her*, no one else. *It's nothing personal* was how Molly's mother often responded when Molly described some stinging slight, some injustice. As if that lessened the hurt. But this was totally personal. Molly knew what it meant. She remembered that look on Lloyd Coleman's face.

"It's a hate crime," Celia said. "That's what it is."

"They do hate me, don't they?" Molly said, and her voice broke. "They want to void *my* contract." Celia patted her arm, but she didn't disagree.

"What did I ever do to them?" Molly asked.

"Nothing," Celia said. "Not a darn thing."

"It's nothing I did, is it?" Molly said. "It's who I am."

Celia must have gathered her thoughts after that. By lunchtime she was ready to weigh in. She was angry and indignant and not about to hold back.

"They are such cowards," she announced. "Gutless. That's what they are. Gutless."

Molly just nodded.

"It doesn't take much courage to vandalize a locker," Celia said. "They never quite got around to signing their names, did they?"

She was speaking so loud, Molly was afraid they'd be overheard. Lloyd and his crew were at the far end of the cafeteria, but still, Molly wondered, why broadcast? It crossed her mind that maybe Celia *wanted* to be overheard. Probably not. Probably it was just Celia being Celia, blasting away on her tuba, playing a solo in the key of outrage.

" 'Give it up'?" Celia said, and snorted. "I mean, is that their best stuff? That's it? That's their A-game?"

Molly had to agree. It was pretty lame.

"You know what it sounds like to me?" Celia said. " 'Surrender Dorothy.' Do you remember that scene in *The Wizard of Oz*? The witch riding her broomstick in the sky above the Emerald City, writing her message in smoke?"

Molly smiled. It was funny to think of Lloyd Coleman riding a broomstick. But what wasn't funny was the prospect of seeing him that afternoon at practice. Thanks to him, she had a painful purple welt on her shin. There was no telling what he would try next. There were plenty of ways you could hurt someone in baseball. Balls, bats, cleats—you could turn anything into a weapon. Who was going to watch her back?

"Dorothy had Toto," Molly said. "I feel like I'm in this all alone."

"You could get a dog," Celia said.

"My mom's allergic," Molly said.

"Figures."

"Dorothy also had the Scarecrow," Molly said. "Don't forget about that. She had the Tin Man."

"You've got me," Celia said. "You've got Jackie Mitchell."

"Plus," Molly said, "Dorothy had ruby slippers."

"You don't need ruby slippers," Celia said.

"Oh, I don't, do I?" Molly said. "Personally, I think I could use a little magic."

"You've got your own," Celia said. "You've got your own kind of magic."

While she was putting on her cleats that afternoon, Molly thought about Jackie Mitchell. She struck out Babe Ruth! It was mind-boggling. The greatest home-run hitter who ever lived. Probably he was expecting fastballs, Molly figured, and Jackie gave him something off-speed. She must have outsmarted him. Molly would have loved to have seen it, the Bambino whiffing in grand style, screwing himself into the ground. And then she was banned from baseball, blacklisted.

And Molly thought about what Celia had said about magic. When she was a little girl, her dad used to read to her from a big book of fairy tales. These were the real thing, Grimm, not Disney. And some of them *were* grim. Her mother disapproved: "Such stuff! You'll give the poor girl nightmares." But Molly loved them, the stranger the better. There was darkness and death and plenty of wickedness, sure, but it was no worse than the nightly news. And there was magic, too—spells and powers, transformations and wishes granted. That was what Molly loved, what she remembered best about those stories. When Cinderella planted a branch on her mother's grave and watered it with her tears, a magic tree grew.

64

9. SECRET SOCIETY

"There's a boy at the door," Molly's mother shouted up the stairs at her. It was Saturday morning, almost eleven. Molly had been lying on her bed, paging through a thick biography of Abraham Lincoln, the book her dad had been reading back in October, the book he'd never finished. She'd rescued it from a box on the back porch. She'd been studying pictures of Lincoln but thinking about her dad.

"Molly," her mother said again. "There's a boy at the door." She stressed the word "boy," and her voice had such a weird intonation, it sounded like some kind of crazy coded message. Those were the first words spoken to her that day. It was such an odd thing to say—a boy at the door? For a moment Molly couldn't understand what it meant or how she was supposed to respond. What exactly are you supposed to do about a boy at the door?

She took a quick glance in the mirror and didn't much like what she saw there. She hardly ever did. She gave her hair a couple of quick brushes and tied it back in a tight ponytail, the way she fixed her hair under a baseball cap. But it didn't make much difference, one way or another. In the mirror there was still a plain-faced, apprehensive-looking girl. Molly stuck her tongue out at her and headed downstairs.

Turned out "a boy at the door" meant Lonnie House, who was sitting on her front steps. An old, blue, fat-tired bicycle was kick-standed behind him in the driveway. At first Molly thought that Lonnie must have been riding by and got a flat, that he needed some roadside assistance. He looked slumped and stranded. But it was hard to tell: He always looked a little bit stranded.

"Lonnie," Molly said.

She looked and saw that his tires were fully inflated. So this wasn't an accident after all—it was a social call.

Lonnie was wearing jeans, a big T-shirt, high-tops, his usual getup, but today he looked better put together than usual somehow. Molly couldn't put her finger on it exactly.

"So did Niedermeyer torture you?" Molly asked Lonnie. She hadn't had a chance to talk to him since the locker thing. "Did he give you detention?"

"Nah," Lonnie said. "I got a warning."

"Just a warning?"

"A *stern* warning," Lonnie said, and smiled. "I had to promise never to draw on lockers again. Or else."

Molly had been a little disappointed when she'd discovered that while she was in class, someone on the maintenance staff had cleaned off Lonnie's mural. There were a few black smudges remaining, a couple of stray lines, which cheered her up while she dialed the numbers of her combination. She could imagine the rest. "It was a great picture," Molly said.

"Kind of a rush job," Lonnie said. "I could've done better with more time."

There was a pause. Then Lonnie pointed to his baseball glove, which he'd looped over the handlebars of his bike.

"I thought maybe we could practice a little," he said. "Not that you need it or anything."

"Oh, I need it," Molly said. "Practice is just what I need."

Molly led Lonnie around the side of the house into the backyard. She opened the garage door and grabbed her glove and a ball. Molly went to her usual place, and Lonnie gravitated unknowingly to her dad's old spot, positioning himself the right distance from her, the distance between the pitcher's mound and home plate, right where her dad used to stand.

At that point Molly realized why Lonnie looked different—his hair was combed. That was it. Molly liked him fluffy just fine, but it was touching, almost, to think of him running a comb through his hair on her account.

They tossed the ball back and forth easily, nice and slow, and Molly was grateful that it wasn't necessary to say anything. Small talk, especially with a boy, sometimes seemed impossible. Last September Brett Sparks, a boy from her homeroom, had invited her to meet him for a bagel. He seemed like a nice kid, but their meeting had been an ordeal. What killed her were the silences. She'd racked her brain, come up with some questions, a couple of reasonably interesting observations, and what she got back were mono-syllables—"yes," "no," "yeah." It was horrible.

Here, with Lonnie, tossing the ball, they were making some noise, the ball was popping in their gloves. They weren't just *staring* at each other, stiff as a couple of man-nequins. With Brett, Molly had felt like a complete dork, awkward and nervous. Something as simple as a swallow of chocolate milk or a bite of bagel and cream cheese seemed like humiliation-waiting-to-happen. But with a glove on her hand, Molly knew how to act, she felt like herself.

Molly mixed in one knuckler. It took a little dip and Lonnie nabbed it deftly on one hop. He grinned. "Let's see that again," he said.

Molly's mother appeared in the kitchen window. Molly remembered that night when she'd come out all by herself and hatched her scheme while watching her mother through the same window. Molly suspected that her mother ap-proved of her having a visitor. A boy at the door would be a good thing in her eyes, evidence that Molly was normal or maybe even popular. But she'd want it all done the right way. Her mother believed in propriety, etiquette, proper channels, meeting the parents. She'd want to do a back-ground check on any boy Molly was interested in.

A couple of pitches caromed off his glove, a few skipped past him entirely, but Lonnie didn't seem the least bit upset about it. He'd retrieve the ball, toss it back, and get ready for the next pitch. The longer they threw, the fewer he missed.

After a while, once she'd broken a sweat, Molly let

Lonnie know that she was ready for a break. She held up her hand. "Enough for now," she said.

There were a couple of plastic lawn chairs on the back deck, and Molly waved him over. They settled in like a couple of oldsters, staring out across the lawn. This was her deck, her lawn. It was where she'd sat hundreds of times, watching her dad grill burgers, eating her mom's potato salad off a paper plate. Sitting here with Lonnie, though, it looked different—not better, not worse, just different.

Lonnie asked how long she'd been throwing the knuckler, and she told him just a little about playing catch with her dad. He wanted to know how she gripped it, and she showed him. Molly was a little embarrassed by her unglamorous hands, her stubby fingers on the ball, her chewed-up nails. But Lonnie was a kid who wrote on his hands, not just a phone number or address but strings of words, long lines of tiny blue text filling the back of his hand, full sentences probably. It was a running joke at school—"Hey, House, ever hear of paper?" He didn't have much ground to be judgmental about her need for a manicure.

Lonnie leaned forward, squinting a little, studying her grip with the same sort of concentration he had devoted to the composition of his locker mural. He was an artist, Molly supposed; he was into technique, he was all about how-to.

Lonnie seemed so genuinely interested in what she had to say, Molly told him more. She shared some of the knuckleball lore her father had passed along to her over the years. She told him how a guy named Paul Richards invented a special oversized floppy mitt to make catching a knuckler a little bit easier.

"I could use one of those," Lonnie said.

She told him about the masters: Hoyt Wilhelm, Wilbur Wood, the Niekro brothers. She explained that in honor of Wilhelm, most knuckleball pitchers chose to wear the same uniform number, 49, Wilhelm's age when he retired.

"It's like a club," Lonnie said.

"I guess it is."

"A secret society," Lonnie said.

"Something like that," Molly said.

They sat there for a moment, not saying anything. Lonnie took the ball from Molly and slowly arranged his fingers into the knuckleball grip she'd demonstrated, not perfect, but pretty close. He'd been paying attention.

"You really miss your dad," Lonnie said. He said it quietly, almost to himself, but Molly heard him, loud and clear.

It was so simple, so true. Molly felt it like a punch in the gut. All of a sudden there was something happening in her chest, something behind her eyes.

Molly already knew that she was going to tell Celia this story—the boy at the door, their baseball date. It would make a good story. Celia would appreciate it. But Molly understood that when she told it, she was going to leave some things out. She would leave out the part when she started crying. She wouldn't try to describe the way her shoulders shook, how Lonnie took her hand and held it tight, not patting, not rubbing, just a good firm grip, how he waited quietly while she regained her composure.

It wasn't that she didn't trust Celia. But some things couldn't be put into words. What happened to her insides when Lonnie mentioned her dad. It was sorrow. It was grief. It was what your body felt when it knew the sad truth.

Molly would tell Celia they'd talked some more, but she'd be vague about the details. She wouldn't pass along what Lonnie told her about missing his own father. His wasn't dead but divorced, living in a new house in a distant suburb with a new wife and a new baby, a new car, everything so sparkling and perfect that he and his mother now seemed shabby in comparison. They seemed like an embarrassing mistake, the first draft of a life his father had discarded.

That was private. That was between the two of them. It was something he had entrusted to her, and she intended to be worthy of it.

10. A ZEN THING

On Monday morning, in homeroom, Celia gave Molly something. It was a thin, beat-up paperback book. About Zen and the art of archery.

"You need to read this," Celia said.

"Archery?" Molly said. "As in bows and arrows?"

"You need to read this," Celia said.

"As in Robin Hood? You're kidding, right?"

"Molly," Celia said. Her tone of voice was kindly but stern. It was how you'd talk to a naughty toddler or a wild puppy. "You need to read this."

"Because . . ."

"You need to read it," Celia said, "because you need to read it. Trust me. It's a Zen thing."

Later that morning, during study hall, when she probably should have been doing a math worksheet, Molly took a look at the book. There were loose pages and passages underlined in red and blue. The paper was yellowed with age. Probably it had belonged to Celia's brother Michael, who was currently or used to be a Buddhist.

The book was about a guy who goes to Japan to study Zen. But you don't just study Zen; you don't just read a book or take a class. You have to learn to do something, to master some kind of art—flower arranging, drinking tea (according to the book, drinking tea could be an art), archery, whatever. You have to devote yourself. It didn't matter what you did, what mattered was how you did it. And to learn to do it right apparently took a long time. The author of the book seemed to have practiced with a master for years—years!—before he made much progress with his bow and arrow. A lot of it sounded like gibberish, like New Age babble: Consciousness and Unconsciousness, Emptiness, Illumination, Oneness, Artless Art.

But by the time the bell rang, Molly had at least figured out where Celia was coming from. Baseball might be like archery. The real contest was with yourself. That's what the book said. Throwing a knuckleball might be like shooting an arrow. There was a target you were trying to hit, but you didn't just aim and fire—it was more complicated than that.

Last Friday, Molly had been a little afraid to return to practice after the locker incident. She was worried about what Lloyd and his gang were going to do, how they planned to target her next. But they were apparently lying low, at least for now. That afternoon and throughout this week, they didn't aim anything at her.

Today Molly noticed Lloyd and Lonnie talking before practice. They were sitting on the bench together, their heads turned toward each other. Molly was too far away to hear what they were saying. She couldn't imagine what the two of them had to talk about. It wasn't like they were friends. "What was that about?" she'd asked him later while they were shagging balls in the outfield. "You and Lloyd?" Was Lloyd giving Lonnie a hard time about his drawing? Lonnie telling Lloyd to back off? Lonnie wasn't talking. "Nothing" was all he said. "It was about nothing."

Molly thought she seemed a little less invisible to some of the other boys. During warm-ups she retrieved a ball for James Castle, and he thanked her. When it was time for pitchers and catchers to work, Ben Malone let her know. "Hey, Williams," he'd said. "Coach wants us." She liked to think that maybe she had earned some respect by not cowering, by just coming back for more.

Molly noticed things had changed somehow between her and Lonnie. Neither mentioned his Saturday visit, their game of catch and their conversation afterward. But things had shifted. For one thing, when it was time to pair up and play catch, they immediately found each other. No milling around, no questions asked.

As part of her little lecture on the history of the knuckleball, Molly had explained to Lonnie how many knuckleball pitchers came to have one catcher who specialized in catching that pitch for that particular pitcher. In the 1960s a guy named J. C. Martin made a living catching the great Hoyt

Wilhelm's knuckleball. Doug Mirabelli always caught Tim Wakefield and his knuckleball for the Red Sox. They were called "personal catchers." Catching a knuckleball was so difficult and so unpleasant for most regular catchers that if you could do it reasonably well (nobody did it really well), that one skill could keep you on the team. The personal catcher would sit on the bench until the knuckleballer took the mound, and then he and his special floppy mitt would enter the game. It was an odd kind of intimacy, to be joined together like that, a weird baseball marriage.

During this week of practice it became clear that Lonnie had become Molly's personal catcher. Nobody said it, but everyone understood. During the second half of each practice, pitchers and catchers split from the rest of the squad, and Lonnie and Molly always worked together. That was fine with her. Lonnie had even acquired a catcher's mitt of his own. It looked new, or newish. Molly didn't ask, and Lonnie didn't tell. It somehow seemed too personal to mention.

Though he didn't look like anybody's idea of an all-star ballplayer, Lonnie was getting good at catching the knuckler. Molly liked throwing to him. Maybe it was because he seemed so fearless, so unflappable. Nothing fazed him. He never flinched. Molly had seen a couple of baseball-sized bruises on his arms, but he never complained. If a pitch got by him, he didn't grouse about it, he just retrieved it. When Lonnie was catching, he sometimes made that same humming sound as when he was drawing. Molly believed he probably wasn't even aware of it himself; it was just how he concentrated. When she looked in and saw him—crouched and ready, masked and padded, but underneath it all, still Lonnie, hair sticking out—it calmed her down.

On Wednesday night Molly got home before her mother and decided to just go ahead and fix her own dinner. It seemed like a good idea at the time. A way to declare her independence. But things weren't going well. There'd been some mishaps. By the time her mother came through the door, there was a blackened pan soaking in the sink, cheesy debris all over the countertop, a melted spatula in the garbage, and the smell of burned oil in the air.

Over the years Molly had watched her dad make plenty of omelets, and so imagined she could whip one up for herself tonight, no problem. How hard could it be?

Her dad liked to talk while he cooked. He recited little rules of thumb, cooking theories and principles, which Molly thought she remembered. Hot pan, cold oil. He was always saying that. Or was it cold pan, hot oil? Both sounded true. Her dad used to say you should cook eggs at the lowest possible temperature. Or was it the highest?

And who knew there were so many kinds of oil? Vegetable, corn, olive, flavored and unflavored. Molly opted for olive oil, which sounded healthy, but while it was heating in her dad's favorite skillet, she got focused on beating eggs and grating cheese. She was wondering if cooking could be a Zen art, too, if maybe she could find illumination in the kitchen.

Next thing Molly knew, the smoke alarm was beeping, a spatula, which she'd left too close to the burner, was melting down, and her pan was an evil-looking, scorched mess.

Of course that was when her mother came in the door. She surveyed the scene, quietly assessed the damage. Molly had turned on the fan and disengaged the alarm, but still. It looked pretty bad. But Molly's mother didn't lecture or scold. She didn't say much of anything at all. She grabbed a dishcloth and helped Molly clean up.

They worked together for a while in silence before her mother finally spoke. "Lonnie seems like a nice boy," she said. It was a holdover remark from Saturday—her mother was apparently still puzzling over the boy at the door.

Molly had dodged her mother's questions the day of Lonnie's visit the best she could, provided only the minimal background data. She'd told her that he was in Honors, which was both true and just the sort of thing she would like, and that they both liked to play ball, which was basically true, too.

"Yes," Molly said. She was sometimes afraid that everything she said to her mother could and would eventually be used against her. So she found ways to be pleasant but to divulge as little as possible. "He is a very nice boy."

"So," her mother said. She was rinsing her hands in the sink with a kind of studied nonchalance. "You two are going out." It was a classic interrogation technique: She wasn't asking a question, just floating an incriminating statement and then waiting for confirmation. It was how they sometimes coaxed confessions from murderers on TV cop shows: *So then you killed her.*

"Mom," Molly said. She tried to sound just a little exasperated, pained but patient, willing to school her mother. "Nobody does that anymore. People don't 'go out.' They don't exchange rings and go steady. We're just friends, boys and girls, we hang out together, all of us. Lonnie's my friend."

When Molly heard herself say that—"Lonnie's my friend"—it sounded surprisingly true. She was pretty sure she liked the sound of it.

"Of course," her mother said, and dried her hands. When she felt dated, she would usually back off. Molly didn't enjoy making her mother feel old and out of it, but it worked. Right now she was willing to do what she had to in order to protect her privacy.

Once the kitchen had been restored to order, they made themselves sandwiches, peanut butter on whole wheat. Molly poured a couple of glasses of milk and they ate at the kitchen table.

"How was practice?" her mother asked.

Molly knew her mother meant softball, the girls' team, but she hadn't said that, not specifically. "Fine," Molly said.

Technically, she was telling the truth, but she felt like she was lying, and she didn't like the sensation. She felt guilty being deceptive. But she didn't feel ready to go there, not yet, not with her mother. Molly didn't know what words she would even use to explain what she was doing.

When she first went out for baseball, she'd talked to Tess Warren about it. Molly was a little afraid that her softball friends might be hurt that she'd abandoned the team. Rejected them somehow. What Molly said came out part explanation, part apology. "Go for it" was what Tess said. She didn't sound cold exactly, but she didn't sound all that warm either.

When Molly tried to imagine telling her mother, it came

out sounding stupid. Maybe it *was* stupid. So Molly took a big bite of her sandwich, filled her mouth with peanut butter, nodded, and made some agreeable noise.

On Friday, for the first time, Molly threw to hitters in a scrimmage. The batters wore helmets. On the bench players spit sunflower seeds nervously and kept their eyes glued to what was happening on the field. There was no joking around. Everyone understood that what happened could decide who made the team and who got cut.

Coach V stood behind the mound and called balls and strikes. Molly knew some of the boys thought he was just a weird old guy. They rolled their eyes behind his back. They called him "Gramps." There were rumors about him. Who was he, anyway? some of the boys wanted to know. Why didn't he use his full name? What was he hiding? He was a Cuban defector, somebody said, a former Olympic ballplayer who floated into Miami on a raft. Somebody else said he was a criminal, and this was his court-ordered community service.

Molly tried to think of him as a Zen master, a teacher trained in the old ways, a sensei, someone whose long experience was worthy of respect. He didn't say much, but when he did, it often had that slow-burning Zen quality. It would be something you might have to take some time and think about.

Molly got off to a shaky start. Her first knuckleball didn't knuckle at all: it spun rather than floated, and Ryan Vogel, her bad-breathed saxophone buddy, hit it to left field for a solid single. She walked the next batter on four straight pitches, all knuckleballs, none of them close to being strikes. She threw one decent floater to Lloyd Coleman, who swung under it and popped out softly to the second baseman, but then she got wild again and walked another batter.

Bases loaded now and one out. If Lonnie let a ball get past now, a run would score. The pressure was on both of them. Molly took a deep breath and tried to recall the lessons she'd been reading in her Zen book. In archery the secret was letting go. There was a whole chapter about that. Shooting an arrow was not about gritting your teeth and trying hard. Neither was throwing a knuckleball. It wasn't about getting mad or all pumped up and red faced, none of that kill-kill football mentality. *Don't think*, the master says. *Be like a child.*

"Just play catch," Desmond Davis hollered at Molly from shortstop. Desmond was probably the best athlete on the team, fast and strong with a rocket arm. He was quiet, not shy but self-contained. He mostly kept to himself. It pleased Molly that he would offer some encouragement. "Just play catch."

It was a baseball cliché, one of the oldest. It was what you said to a wild pitcher. But this time Molly heard it, really heard it, for the first time maybe, and realized it was great advice, brilliant even. The batter didn't have to be part of the equation. In the backyard, that was what Molly had done with her dad, she'd just played catch. The batters were imaginary, so they never bothered or distracted or frightened her.

Molly played catch with Lonnie. She threw two knucklers

for called strikes, one for a ball, and then one more that the batter swung at and missed. The pitch did a little hop at the end, but Lonnie held on. Two outs.

"That's the way!" Desmond hollered. "That's how it's done."

Next up was Grady Johnston. Molly had known him forever. She remembered that in the third grade they sat at the same table and once worked together to make up a secret code, a complicated bunch of numbers and letters they used to spell out their names. These days he was all attitude and posture. Sometimes Molly would walk past Grady and his pals on the school lawn, and they'd be draped across their bicycles like little hoodlums in training, smirking and swearing, whispering and pointing at girls.

Now, at the plate, Grady was energetically chewing a big wad of bubble gum. He pawed at the dirt and tugged at his batting gloves. When he finally assumed his stance, his bat kept moving in tight, menacing circles.

"That boy looks awfully eager," Coach V said.

Molly knew it wasn't about eagerness. It wasn't about bluster. It was about waiting. She decided to make Grady wait a little longer. She motioned for Lonnie to join her on the mound for a conference.

Lonnie pushed his mask off his face and Molly noticed some fresh writing on the back of his hand. It was practically covered in blue ink, not just a word or a phrase, but long lines of tiny letters, whole sentences. It looked like a paragraph—it could have been the first chapter of a novel.

"Aren't you afraid of ink poisoning?" Molly asked.

"Everybody asks that," Lonnie said.

"I wonder why."

"Ink isn't poisonous," he said.

"You better hope not."

Molly was trying to read his hand, but it wasn't easy to do, not upside down, written across the contours of his skin. But she saw her name. *Maybe* it was her name, or something like it. But that's all. She couldn't make out the rest. If it was in a full sentence, and she was the subject, she didn't know the predicate. How did she feel about that? Her name on his skin. She wasn't sure.

"Okay," Coach V said. "Enough chitchat. How about we play ball?"

Lonnie resumed his position behind the plate, and Grady stepped into the box, still chewing and twitching and tugging and waggling.

Lonnie asked for a knuckleball, and Molly gave him one. This one came in high but dropped into the strike zone.

Coach V raised his right hand. "One," he said.

Grady kept up his little ritual of digging and wagging. It was what her science teacher called display behavior: what an animal does to show off and to appear fierce. A guy like Grady was all about display. Molly tried her best to ignore him. She was just playing catch. Her second pitch did a little wiggle and came in over the outside corner.

Coach V raised his right hand once more. "Two," he said.

Be like a child, Molly told herself. She ignored Grady. She looked at Lonnie's mitt and imagined it was her dad's big floppy Wilson. She imagined she was in her backyard on a summer day feeling happy and carefree. She didn't aim, she just wound up and let the ball go.

If it were possible for a pitched baseball to have a sense of humor, this one did. It came in belt high, nice and slow, right over the middle of the plate. It looked like the fattest, juiciest pitch imaginable. That was the setup of the joke it was going to tell.

Grady's eyes got big. He lunged forward and took a huge swing. But while Grady was lurching forward, the pitch delivered the punch line of its little joke. It veered off toward Grady's shoe tops, where Lonnie scooped it up on one hop just as Grady was following through from his mighty whiff.

Grady stood frozen for a moment, as if stunned. Coach V raised his thumb in the air—"Batter's out," he said matter-of-factly—and Lonnie stood up, a big grin on his face.

Grady came to then. He looked a little wild. He ripped the batting helmet off his head and sailed it in the general direction of the bench. It bounced and skidded toward Coach Morales, who was standing there alone, his arms folded across his chest.

Morales calmly stepped aside and watched while the helmet spun and came to rest in the dirt.

"All right," he said. "I've seen enough."

11. GLOW-IN-THE-DARK STARS

*F*riday night Molly babysat for the Rybaks, the family next door. Even though she'd done it many times before and knew the drill, Mrs. Rybak ran through her excruciatingly detailed list of instructions and list of telephone numbers. Molly knew Kyle was allergic to walnuts, she knew Caitlin's bedtime was eight o'clock. They were just going to dinner and a movie, but Molly got the full briefing. She nodded attentively and responsibly. She liked Caitlin and Kyle, and liked the extra money, and she really liked the chance to be out of her house for a while, if only next door.

As soon as the Rybaks left, Kyle hunkered down with his Game Boy, and Caitlin dragged Molly off into her room to play Pretty Pretty Princess. It was a dress-up board game, like Candy Land, only with plastic jewelry, which players earned, piece by piece—rings, bracelets, earrings. Caitlin never got tired of it. She could play Pretty Pretty Princess all night. For Molly the fun of the game was watching Caitlin's face: how excited she was to put on a bracelet, how solemn she looked when she won a game and put on the cardboard crown. Molly liked lying on her belly on the carpeted floor of Caitlin's pink girly-girl room. She could be as silly or as stupid as she liked. It was like being on vacation from her real life, her serious self. No one was watching her, no one was grading her, no one was judging her.

After she performed the bedtime routines with the kids—bath, snack, and books—Molly went downstairs and called Celia.

"What's the food situation there?" Celia wanted to know. "Have you looked in the fridge yet?"

Molly walked the phone into the kitchen and looked around. A bowl of fruit on the counter, jars of pasta, milk and yogurt and eggs in the refrigerator. Nothing unusual.

"You know what I like to do when I sit?" Celia asked. "I pig out on the kids' cereal. Cap'n Crunch, Frosted Flakes, anything with those little marshmallows."

"You do?" Molly couldn't believe it. Celia scarfing up Lucky Charms? It seemed so unlikely. "You? Miss Health Food?"

"You know why?" Celia asked. "Nostalgia. Other than the smell of Play-Doh, cereal is the fastest way to bring back childhood. One taste of Cocoa Puffs and I'm a little kid again. It's a blast from the past."

"My mom wouldn't buy me sugary cereals," Molly said.

"All the more reason then to dig in and taste the forbidden fruit," Celia said. "But you better be careful."

"What are you talking about?"

"You might OD on all that sugar," Celia said. "If you've never done Trix before, you might start to hallucinate. The toaster might talk to you. You might think you can fly."

"If I do," Molly said, "I'll call you."

"You do that," Celia said. "I'll talk you down."

Later, when Molly looked in on Caitlin, she remembered what Celia had said about childhood. For Molly, the feeling didn't come in a cereal box or a can of modeling clay. For her, it was right there in Caitlin's little-girl room: the canopy bed, the frilly pillows, the glow-in-the-dark stars on her ceiling, her collection of stuffed bears and poodles. Molly's childhood bedroom had looked different—not so pink, not so frilly. But it *felt* the same, just as safe and secure and carefree. Caitlin was sound asleep. Molly had heard the phrase "not a care in the world" and understood now what it meant. It was in the rhythm of Caitlin's breath. Molly envied her a little: her innocence, her cocooned, protected happiness, which she did not appreciate, which you could not possess and appreciate at the same time. To love it, you first had to lose it.

Molly looked out Caitlin's window and saw the blinking red light of a radio tower in the distance. When she was a little girl, she used to watch that same red light outside her own bedroom window. She remembered that sometimes she used to make a wish—not on a star, the way you were supposed to, but on that stupid light. What did she wish for?

She couldn't remember. Did her wishes come true? They must not have.

From Caitlin's window, Molly could see her own house. It looked serene and safe. There was a light on in the family room, a light shining in the kitchen. It could be where a happy television family lived, a place where all problems could be solved within thirty minutes.

Molly saw her mother's figure cross by the kitchen window. And then she was standing at the sink, rinsing a dish. From her perch at Caitlin's window, Molly could see her mother plain as day. She wasn't that far away from her. Molly tried to think of her mother neutrally, objectively. What if she were not her mother? What if she were just the woman next door? At this distance, from this perspective, she seemed smaller somehow, less intimidating, less annoying. Less everything. She looked tired. Her head was bobbing a little, as if she might be humming a tune. What song would her mother hum? Molly had no idea. There was a lot she didn't know about her.

Molly impulsively knocked on Caitlin's window. "Mom?" she said. "Mom!" But her mother couldn't hear her. Molly watched as her mother stepped away from the sink and turned off the light.

Downstairs, Molly walked through the house and listened to its foreign noises. The hum of the fridge, the whir of the dishwasher in the dry cycle, a clock ticking somewhere. She decided to give Lonnie a call. She didn't have anything particular to say, she just wanted to hear a friendly voice. Lonnie's mother answered, sounding exhausted and frazzled.

With her impeccable telephone manners drilled into her by her mother, Molly identified herself and asked whether she might please speak to Lonnie. Mrs. House muttered something that Molly couldn't make out and set the phone down. There was a television playing in the background, something loud and possibly angry, something that definitely didn't sound educational or informative.

"Hey, Lonnie," Molly said when he picked up. "It's me."

"I guess the mighty Grady struck out," Lonnie said.

"He wasn't too happy, was he?"

"You should have seen him in the locker room."

"No thanks."

"Monday is when Coach is gonna post the list," Lonnie said.

"I know," Molly said.

"Are you worried?"

"I'm trying to not think about it." Of course, Molly didn't say, it was impossible to not think about something. The harder you tried, the more you thought about it.

There was some background noise on Lonnie's end, an unhappy voice. It might have been the television, it might have been Lonnie's mother. Reality TV, or maybe just reality. Molly felt bad for Lonnie, but what could she do? The show he was living in was a complicated mess. "I'll let you go," she said. "See you Monday."

"Fingers crossed," Lonnie said.

The house was quiet now, the kids were asleep. The toys were picked up and put away. In the family room, Molly flicked on the television and cranked herself back in Mr.

Rybak's recliner. It reminded her of being at the dentist. She tried one of the beanbags, where Kyle and Caitlin watched their cartoons and Disney videos. She slid off at first, and though she finally managed to get perched on one of them, she just couldn't get comfortable. She felt like Goldilocks. In the Rybaks' house she was a restless intruder.

There was a big wooden desk with a rolling chair. Molly tried that. She took a seat and immediately felt important. She could imagine making major decisions here, paying some big bills. There was a leather blotter on the top of the desk, file-cabinet drawers built into the sides.

She pulled open a drawer and took a peek. There was a yellow envelope of family photographs and some paperwork for appliances, instructions and warranties. Some bills and bank statements.

Molly didn't mean to snoop. It didn't occur to her that the Rybaks harbored any secrets. They were an all-American family. Their life was an open book.

She didn't think she was looking for anything. And then she found it: her dad's obituary cut from the newspaper. Already it looked old, aged, historical. Was it a tribute to her dad that the Rybaks saved it, or just an oversight?

Along with the story, there was a photograph of her dad, which Molly didn't like. Her mother had insisted on a closed casket at the funeral, wanting, Molly assumed, to spare them all the pain of seeing his lifeless face. But in this obituary photograph he looked lifeless, too. He was smiling, but in a stiff, unnatural way. It was like a bad school portrait. He was wearing a tie. That's not how he looked, Molly thought, not how he smiled. She was afraid to look at it for too long. She didn't want it to replace the pictures in her head, her memory's snapshots of how he really smiled. His crooked grin when she used to tell him the kind of corny jokes he never tired of. The conspiratorial smile when he and Molly pulled something over on her mother—when he'd slip her an extra cookie or spring her from bedtime to watch the last few innings of a ballgame with him. When he smiled for real, his eyes got narrow and his nose crinkled.

Molly's name was in the article: she was the daughter he was survived by. It was probably written by one of his friends from the newspaper, maybe his best pal, Milt Hedstrum, whom Molly had always called Uncle Milt. At the wake he had looked so broken down and red eyed, Molly had felt the urge to comfort him. The obituary reported the fact that her dad had died in a single-car accident. It was a phrase Molly had heard repeated again and again at the time of her dad's death. When she heard someone say it, "single-car accident," it sounded sinister and secretive. It was like a message in a code she could never crack.

12. ABRAHAM LINCOLN'S EYES

*T*hat night Molly dreamed about her father again. He was dressed in the shirt and tie he wore in the obituary picture, and Molly understood that he was dead. His eyes were open, he was alert, he was seated at some sort of desk, but he was dead. Molly knew it just by looking at him. She knew it in that way you know something in a dream. His eyes were huge and mournful. They were Abraham Lincoln's eyes.

She understood what a terrible thing it was to be dead. All this time she'd been thinking only of herself. How much she missed him, how hard it was not to have him in her life. But she'd never really given any thought to her dad. At the funeral the preacher said he'd gone to a better place. But in

Molly's dream he did not seem to be in a better place at all. He was seated stiffly in some chokingly formal pseudo living room. It was not a place where someone actually lived. It was more like a furniture store display, or a stage set. There was dark carpeting and heavy curtains. It was the funeral home, Molly realized.

Molly wanted to speak to her dad, she wanted to hear him speak. No matter what he might say, she wanted to hear the sound of his voice. In the early days and weeks after his death, she'd been able to hear his voice clearly in her head. Lately, though, she was afraid that it had faded away.

It was hard for her to speak. It was as if her mouth were full of Novocain. But finally she was able to get something out. "Dad?" she said. "Dad!"

She waited for her father to respond. To hear his voice. She stared into his face, into those sorrowful eyes. She understood somehow that he wanted to say something but couldn't. He stood slowly. He was a tall man, a shade over six feet, and now, in her dream, he seemed even taller. Her father turned suddenly and, with two quick, graceful strides, disappeared behind a dark curtain.

Molly woke up shaky, her heart pounding. As a little girl, she'd had her share of nightmares, dreams of monsters and skeletons, dreams of being chased, dreams of falling. This was quieter, but more disturbing. It felt hushed, but final.

At breakfast, Molly kept thinking about her dream. She couldn't shake that image of her dad. She couldn't forget the depthless sadness in his eyes.

"Mom," Molly said.

Her mother was standing at the kitchen counter, her back to Molly, carefully preparing the one perfect cup of coffee she drank each day, carefully pouring hot water through a cone-shaped filter into her mug. It was a daily ritual that seemed to require a great deal of concentration. "What, honey?" she said. "What is it?"

What is *it*? Molly didn't really know. She didn't know how to say *it*, whatever *it* was. And what was her mother going to do about *it*?

"Never mind," Molly said. "Forget about it."

13. TEAM PLAYER

*E*arly Monday morning, before Molly looked at the list, she had a talk with Celia about it. She wanted to be prepared. She wanted to have her philosophy in place.

"No matter what," Molly said, "I'm okay with it." They were in the band room, putting their instruments away.

"You mean, if you don't make the team," Celia said. "If you get cut."

At first Celia hadn't understood the terminology. "Cuts?" she'd asked. "Cuts?" Molly had explained it with a slashing motion across her throat. Like surgical cuts. They removed the lousy players from the body of the team, like warts. Now Celia got it. She understood what was at stake.

94

"Right," Molly said.

"You're not gonna freak out," Celia said. "That's what you're saying. You're not gonna get weird about it."

"Yes," Molly said.

"You're gonna take it in stride," Celia said. "You don't make the team, you're like, whatever."

"Exactly," Molly said.

"You tried," Celia said.

"I gave it my best shot."

"Sure," Celia said. "Maybe it was just not meant to be."

It made Molly a little suspicious that Celia was suddenly so agreeable. It wasn't like her to spout comforting clichés. It wasn't her style to dish out chicken soup for anyone's soul.

As it turned out, Molly was right to distrust her friend's happy talk. In an instant, Celia shifted gears.

"What a crock," Celia said.

"Crock?" Molly said.

"You get cut," Celia said, "you're gonna feel horrible. Might as well admit it."

Molly didn't say anything.

"You want to make the team," Celia said. "You really want to make the team. It's pretty obvious."

"It is?"

"It is," Celia said. "If you want it, say so. It's okay to want something."

"I want it," Molly said quietly.

"Okay," Celia said.

"I'm not looking for the best players," Coach Morales had said more than once. "I'm looking for the best team." He'd pause then, to let that sink in. Molly thought she understood what the coach was getting at. She knew very well how much teamwork baseball involved.

For her dad it was one of the chief attractions of the game. He loved pointing out small, subtle acts of baseball teamwork. One player backing up another. A perfect cutoff. A double play or pickoff play.

In baseball talk, a "team player" described someone whose game was unselfish. Someone who could sacrifice bunt, say—that is, make an out to help the team. A team player does what is necessary to help the team. The muscle-bound superstuds who stood at home plate and admired their own home runs were not team players. A "role player" was someone who could do some small thing to help the team: bunt or steal a base, maybe, play well in the field in the late innings.

Molly knew very well that she wasn't one of the best players. She would never be a star. Her speed was average; at the plate, she could make contact but not hit for power. She was a good bunter, though. And she knew how to throw a knuckleball, which, on a good day, fooled some batters. Was she part of the best team? Would Coach Morales hold it against her that some of the boys resented her? If she was a role player, what was her role? She honestly didn't know.

There was a bunch of boys standing in front of the physical education bulletin board. Even from a distance Molly could read their body language. She saw Grady Johnston slinking away from the board looking crestfallen. She didn't much like him, but she couldn't help but feel sorry for him. For the boys, being on the team was connected to who they were. Were they somebody or not? It meant that much. To Molly, it meant something, too; it meant a lot, but something different.

Meanwhile she watched little Eli Krause, red-haired and freckled, who was a good kid and could run like the wind, but just was not much of a hitter. Molly figured he'd been doomed from the first day they took batting practice. Eli worked his way through the crowd, got close enough to the board, and then suddenly jumped in the air. It was like he'd been shot with electricity. He turned and Molly saw his face. Such a grin! His neck and cheeks were bright red with excitement. Even his hair looked happy.

Lloyd Coleman was standing there, arms folded across his chest, the picture of self-satisfaction. *Yeah, I made the team*, his posture said. *Was there ever any doubt?* Nearby, Desmond Davis gave a sly five on the side to his friend James Castle, another sure bet. They were in, and Molly couldn't blame them for being glad.

Molly felt her heart beating in her chest. So, yes, she had told Celia the truth. She wanted it, she wanted it bad. One Zen book did not rid her of all desire.

She approached the board, and the boys there made room for her. The list was typed, the names in all caps, alphabetically arranged. Molly scanned it, top to bottom. Halfway down, she saw Lonnie's name. So Lonnie made the team! No matter what, even if she got cut, Molly was happy for him. Where was he? Maybe he was counting on her to find out and break the news.

She took a deep breath and then looked. There it was,

at the very bottom of the list, the very last name: Molly Williams. She felt tears in her eyes. There were people looking at her, but she didn't care.

Molly stepped into the nearest rest room and closed herself in a stall. She wanted to see Lonnie and give him a high five, and she wanted to tell Celia, too. Her lucky stone must have worked its magic. But right now she wanted to be alone for just a moment. To let the news sink in.

So, this one time anyway, Molly got what she wanted. She couldn't help but wonder, *Now what? What does it mean to be a part of this team?* Time would tell.

She remembered that night out in the backyard when it came into her head to try baseball. She could still see that magical knuckleball floating through the night sky. She thought about Jackie Mitchell, who struck out Babe Ruth and then got banned from baseball for being a woman. Molly imagined that she would be pleased. And she thought about her mother, who thought she was on the girls' softball team. She would probably think Molly had lost her mind.

She wondered what her dad would have said. Now she would give almost anything just to hear his voice. Like every kid, Molly had always thought her parents' words were endless, infinite. They were drops of water in the ocean. However many flooded over you, there were always more where those came from, right?

But the ocean only seems bottomless, the sky only appears endless. Her father's words had been finite. There had only been so many, and then, no more. There was an end, a last, and then, never again. That was what mortality meant, what she never could have imagined.

What would her dad have said? It grieved her that now she would have to figure it out for herself. Maybe that was the message of her dream, the meaning of his silence. If he was going to speak, she would have to put words in his mouth.

So be it. Okay. She could do this. After a certain point, every kid knows what his parents are going to say. It's what makes them so exasperating—and lovable, too.

Molly, her dad would say, *you done good.* It was how he could be proud but not full of hot air, not embarrassing. He would smile then, that slow, lopsided smile of his. Was *that* what she wanted most of all? To put a smile on her sad dad's face?

14. A LINK IN THE CHAIN

*A*t the beginning of practice that afternoon Coach Morales called them together. There weren't as many now, only fifteen after the cuts. It felt different, less like a crowd. They were no longer a mob. There used to be almost thirty, now their number was just about half of that. Already she understood it would be harder to blend in, to become invisible.

"Look," Morales said. He took hold of Desmond Davis's arm and hooked it around the arm of Eli Krause, who was standing next to him. Molly looked but wasn't sure what exactly she was supposed to see. The two boys made an unlikely pair: Desmond, tall, well muscled, dark skinned; Eli, short, scrawny, glow-in-the-dark fair, and freckled. Desmond looked suspiciously stone-faced, and Eli smiled—he was almost always smiling—but it was a nervous grin. *What's this all about?* he seemed to be wondering. *What's coming next?* Would it be painful, embarrassing?

Morales grabbed onto Lonnie's shirt and pushed him into position next to Eli. Lonnie looked scared. Morales took Lonnie's arm, threaded it through the crook of Eli's, and locked it onto Lonnie's hip. Now the three of them stood there, arm-in-arm-in-arm. After that, Morales hooked James Castle onto Lonnie.

"You see what I'm doing?" Morales asked. Molly nodded. She had absolutely no idea what he was doing. Maybe it was some kind of crazy new drill, maybe it was a freaky team-stretching routine.

Morales kept at it. Before long, he had all of them, the whole team, every one of them who'd survived the cuts, all fifteen, plus two coaches, formed into a circle. Molly herself ended up linked between Coach V and Mario Coppola.

"Look around," Morales said, and Molly did. It was a real assortment of humanity. Everett Sheets, a long-legged, skinny-limbed tree, next to Ben Malone, short and squat, with thick legs and a barrel chest, the catcher who looked like a catcher. There was long-haired Lonnie and buzz-cut Lloyd Coleman, and Ian Meriwether, whose hair was short in the back, long in the front, some kind of inverted mullet, which may have been intentional, maybe just a bad haircut. Molly knew that she looked pretty scruffy herself. They were a bunch of mutts at the pound.

"We're a chain," Morales said. "A human chain. I'm a

link in the chain, and you're a link. There are seventeen links in this chain."

Molly could feel Mario stiffen a little. "Is there a most important link in a chain?" Morales asked. "Is any link a star? Is any link more necessary than any other?"

He paused, and little Eli spoke up. "No?"

Morales smiled a little. "That's right," he said. "No link is a star. Every link is important."

Molly saw Lloyd Coleman give his friend Mario a look, a pained, exasperated look. It was the kind of face you made when your parents told their corny stories about the good old days. Molly understood. The whole idea of a human chain was a little weird, quaint. Easy to laugh at. It was a cliché. Only as strong as the weakest link. Blah, blah, blah. But Coach V's arm was reassuringly solid, and standing so close to him, she could smell him—sweet and pungent, like old-fashioned licorice. In that circle Molly felt something. She felt strong and useful. She felt safe. Connected. She felt like a part of something. She liked being a link in a human chain.

"Do we all have to be best friends?" Morales stopped and looked around. Giving them a chance, maybe, to consider how unlikely, how impossible, it was for the motley members of this particular crew ever to be best friends. "No," he said. "Of course not. But we all have to pull together. We need each other. We're all in this together. We're a family."

This practice session seemed to be conducted at some new level of intensity. It was hard to explain, but it just felt different. More serious. It was as if they'd moved on to the next grade. This was Baseball, the advanced course.

Molly spent most of the practice with the other pitchers—Desmond Davis, Lloyd Coleman, and Ian Meriwether—learning how to cover first base. When a ground ball was hit to the first baseman, and he was too far from the bag to get the runner himself, it was the pitcher's job to cover the base and take the throw.

It sounded simple enough. Molly must have seen it happen in big league games on television a couple of hundred times. It seemed like a routine play. A ho-hum, garden-variety out. But watching it and doing it yourself were two different things entirely. Molly discovered there was more to it than she had imagined. It was not a maneuver Molly had practiced in the backyard with her father. It was all new to her. First, you had to get off the mound in a hurry. If you dawdled, if you even thought about it, it was already too late.

Next, Morales explained, a pitcher shouldn't run directly to the base—because you could collide with the runner. Instead, you had to aim for a spot several yards in front of the bag, then run up the line, parallel with the batter, and take the toss from the first baseman on the run. You had to touch the base and keep moving—it was easy to trip or get stepped on by the runner. The timing had to be perfect. If it worked, if the pitcher was quick, if the throw was where it should be, it was pretty. And if something went wrong, it was a train wreck.

Morales set up a drill so they could practice. The pitchers took turns. Each would throw a pitch home to one of the catchers, Ben or Lonnie, watch Morales hit a grounder to Everett Sheets, who played first, then dash down the line toward first and try to beat one of the boys Morales drafted to serve as the runner.

The first few times, Molly was slow, late getting to the base. "Again," Morales said, not angry, just relentless. It had to be automatic. Your legs needed to react before your brain.

After each of the pitchers had taken a few turns, Lloyd Coleman, standing behind Molly in line, started talking. "A guy who plays sports you call a jock," he said. "Because, you know. The equipment." Lloyd was standing near Desmond and Ian, but they didn't respond.

It was Molly's turn next. She took her position on the rubber and started her windup. Lloyd kept talking. "But what about a girl who wants to be a jock?"

Just as Molly threw home, Lloyd said something else, answered his own question presumably. Molly couldn't make out the words, but his tone was nasty.

Morales rapped a hard grounder to Everett at first. Molly bolted off the mound and saw Everett fumble the ball briefly, then recover. She slowed down as she approached the base.

Somehow they all arrived at the same time: the ball, Molly, and Eli Krause, the runner. As Molly stretched for the high throw, Eli must have hunkered down to protect himself and came in low. He took out her legs, and Molly cartwheeled over the top of him. For that instant, cut loose from the ground, time seemed to slow and she could feel herself flying, she could see the landscape tilt. For that split second, she was Evel Knievel, defying gravity. It was thrilling. Then she came down.

She saw, not stars exactly, but a bright light, and may have even blacked out for a second. She opened her eyes and found herself surrounded. There were faces looking down at her. Her left shoulder and back ached. But most of all she felt embarrassed. She'd managed to make herself a spectacle.

Morales shooed everyone away and attended to Molly. She was breathing in shaky gulps but was able to assure him again and again that she was okay, really okay, really, really okay. But he made her stay on the ground anyway and made small talk with her in a quiet voice. He asked her some simple questions. Her name and the day of the week. Maybe he thought she was concussed, brain damaged.

He let her sit up. "How's Eli?" Molly asked, and Morales told her he was fine, unscathed—she'd gotten the worst of it. She stood slowly with Morales's hand on her elbow, and he led her over to the bench. He got her some water and an ice pack. "I'm okay!" Molly said so emphatically that Morales smiled. He told her to relax, take it easy, and left her to watch the last few minutes of practice.

Molly put the pack to her head. Maybe she was brain damaged. Or maybe she'd been brain damaged when she'd decided to play baseball. What had she been thinking?

On the field Lloyd Coleman seemed to be sneaking glances her way—it looked to Molly as if he was smirking. She remembered his little monologue. What joy he must have felt watching her be upended. She could just imagine his rude commentary.

Molly watched Lonnie, who was catching a pitch from Desmond Davis. Lonnie waited while Morales hit a ground ball, then tossed another ball to him. Lonnie looked at ease and unconcerned, casual even. She felt angry at him— unfairly, probably, but since when is anger fair? How could he resume baseball business as usual while she was sitting there, hurt and humiliated? She wanted something from him. She didn't know what exactly, but something. What good was a personal catcher if he couldn't take care of you when you were bruised?

Morales called an end to practice a few minutes later. The players gathered around him, as always, for a few parting words. Molly stood slowly and walked over and joined the team. Already, after just a few minutes on the sidelines, she felt like an outsider. Everyone else was dusty and sweaty, breathing hard, and she had an ice pack in her hand.

"Okay," Morales said. "Listen up." Ordinarily, Morales made only very brief remarks, telling them what they had done well, what they needed to work on. Today, though, he gave them a little talk, preached a little sermon—about failure.

Morales told them that baseball, more than any other sport, is all about failure. "Nobody goes undefeated in baseball," he said. "It's not like college football." Morales explained that if a batter fails seven times out of ten, then he's among the very best. An all-star. How many times did Babe Ruth strike out? More than a thousand times. Think about that: striking out a thousand times. The greatest pitchers ever have won three hundred games in their careers, but how many did they lose along the way? Hundreds.

Molly knew all this. It was the conventional wisdom. It was the sort of thing announcers would discuss during a rain delay. It had been one of her dad's favorite set pieces.

It was not what Molly wanted to hear. She was in no mood to listen to a hymn to failure. Not while she was still smarting from her fall. Not while she was annoyed with Lonnie. She remembered the human chain they'd formed less than two hours earlier. She remembered how solid she felt, how connected. It had not taken long for that feeling to evaporate, for the chain to fall apart.

*M*olly's mother arrived home later than usual that night. Molly had set up at the kitchen table with her homework and a bag of baby carrots. She'd begun work on her social studies project, which was to invent and describe her own country. It had seemed like a stupid assignment at first, but now Molly was getting into it. She was crunching carrots and sketching a map of her country, and it was taking her mind off what she didn't want to think about.

Molly's country was going to be an island, she knew that much. Her country—the Kingdom of Molly, she was tempted to call it—would be in the Pacific, somewhere between Hawaii and New Zealand. It would be ruled by a girl queen. Sparkling bits of coral would be used as money.

There'd be no written language, no technology. Anything important—laws, history, whatever—would be sung. The national pastime would be a primitive form of baseball played with small coconuts.

Molly's mother came through the door, brisk and cheerful, suspiciously cheerful, a bag of groceries in her arm, a bunch of celery sticking out of the top. "Hi, honey," she practically chirped. She could have been auditioning for some retro sitcom.

Molly looked up from her country. "Hi." Her mother had been to the salon. She'd gotten some color and a new haircut. It was sort of sculpted, casually ragged—a Meg Ryan kind of look.

"How was your day?" her mother asked.

Molly could tell that her mother wanted her to say something about her hair. She had that vacant supermodel look. It was a self-absorbed, how-do-I-look? expression, like someone looking into a mirror. Someone using another person as a mirror. She wanted a compliment. She seemed pathetically eager for attention. But Molly wasn't willing to play that game.

"Would you like some carrots?" Molly said, and pushed them across the table. She didn't want to play girlfriend to her mother. Thanks, but no thanks. Maybe the fact that Molly was eating dinner out of a plastic bag would make her mother feel guilty.

Her mother opened the fridge and started loading it from the grocery bag. She gave her head a little shake. Her mother's birthday was just three days off, Molly remembered, on Saturday. Maybe they'd go out for dinner to celebrate.

No matter what, Molly had to think of a gift for her.

The need to shop for her mother made Molly feel a creeping kind of anxiety and even dread. It was an impossible task. If you asked what she wanted for her birthday—or for Christmas, or Mother's Day, for that matter—she'd smile and say, "Nothing." (What was it that Celia had said? *It's okay to want something.*) Or she'd suggest some loving-mom version of nothing: something homemade, a hug. But it was a trap. When she'd open Molly's sincere offering—a hand-picked bouquet, a hand-lettered poem—her mother would smile and say all the right things, but it seemed like a hollow performance. Whatever she really wanted, this wasn't it. It made Molly feel stupid, like a failure. Once Molly presented her with a book of coupons, for things like breakfast in bed, but she never redeemed a single one of them.

A few days before her mother's birthday, Molly and her dad used to hit the mall together. He seemed as clueless as Molly about what might please her. And he seemed baffled, frightened even, by women's things—perfume, lingerie, jewelry. But somehow they always had fun on these doomed shopping missions. She'd tease her dad by dousing him with perfume or by suggesting that they surprise her mom with something hugely inappropriate. A moped. A set of wrenches. A few rap CDs. They'd eventually choose something innocuously beautiful—a silk scarf, say—and then, relieved, happily off the hook until Mother's Day at least, they'd eat Chinese in the food court. Molly realized that this would be another gloomy first without her dad. She'd have to go it alone this time.

"So, Molly," her mother said. "Guess who I ran into? Lorna Schmidt."

"That's nice," Molly said. She was drawing a river and

didn't look up. The river would divide Upper Molly from Lower Molly and bring fresh water to all her subjects. Lorna Schmidt was the mother of Eva Schmidt, a girl in Molly's grade whom she'd been friends with briefly back in fourth grade. Molly's mother seemed to believe they were still close, and Molly never bothered to set her straight.

"You know what she says to me?"

"What?" Molly said. "What does Lorna Schmidt say to you?"

"She says, 'I hear Molly is really stirring it up at school.' 'Oh,' I say. Stirring it up. I don't know what she's talking about, but I play along. I pretend that I have a daughter who tells me things. A daughter who keeps me in the loop. I pretend that I have a daughter who talks to me while she's out there making waves and stirring it up."

Molly put down her pencil. She could feel her face growing warm. "I have no idea what you're talking about," Molly said, but of course she did. It had only been a matter of time, and now she was busted. Eva Schmidt was a gossip, a girl without a life of her own, who had nothing better to do than entertain her mother with stories of her former friend's goings-on at school.

"Oh really," her mother said. Her mother told her the story she'd gotten from Lorna Schmidt. Call it "Molly Stirs It Up." It was pretty funny, as ludicrous and distorted as what gets announced at the end of a game of telephone, after the long chain of whispers, just about everything lost in translation. Molly would have laughed, except that in this story, she was the main character.

The single accurate fact in the story was that Molly was on the baseball team, the only girl. The rest was embroidery, speculation, buzz. In this version of the story, her playing baseball sounded like some wacky stunt. No mention that she had earned her spot on the team, nothing about striking Grady Johnston out, no suggestion that she might actually be a good ballplayer. There was something catty about it, as if playing baseball were a way to meet boys, as if she were some kind of boy-crazy hussy.

"Why wouldn't you tell me?" her mother asked. "Why don't you talk to me?"

"I was going to tell you," Molly said. "I was just waiting for the right moment. I know how busy you are."

"If you don't talk to me, if you keep secrets from me, how can I trust you?"

"Mom, I've been playing baseball, not shooting heroin."

"I deserve better."

Naturally, Molly didn't say, *it's all about you, what you deserve.*

Molly picked up her colored pencil and went back to tracing the river in her country. She pushed too hard and snapped off the tip. Didn't she deserve better, too?

Molly felt her mother's hand on her shoulder. "Playing baseball won't bring him back," her mother said quietly.

Her mother's touch was kindly, but still Molly recoiled a little. It could go either way.

"I know baseball was special to the two of you," her mother said. "Playing catch. Watching the games on television together. It was sweet. It really was."

Molly despised the word "sweet." She had been on the brink of breaking down, but that one word pulled her back. It was a pat on the head. She loosed herself from her mother's grip.

Her mother said, "Molly, you need to . . ." She paused.

Molly fixed her mother with what she hoped was a glare. *Need to what?* she wondered. Move on? Get over it? If her mother used the word "closure," Molly believed, she would launch herself at her and claw her face.

"What?" Molly demanded. "What do I need to do? I'd really like to know. Please tell me. I'm all ears."

Her mother took her measure. "I'm going to start some dinner. You need to pick up your schoolwork and wash up. That's what you need to do."

Her mother did in fact make dinner, chicken and rice and steamed broccoli, which was a pleasant surprise. They ate, mostly in polite silence. But there was a softness in her mother's manner, a gentleness. She inquired politely whether Molly wanted more of this or that. She refilled her water glass. She smiled.

Molly decided to take advantage of her mother's mood and ask something she'd been stewing about.

"Was he sad?" she asked.

"Your father?"

"Yes," Molly said. "My father. Your husband. Peter J. Williams. Was he sad?"

"Sometimes. Everybody is sad sometimes."

"How sad?"

"There's no Richter scale, Molly. Sometimes he was sad. Mostly he wasn't. Was he depressed? Is that what you're getting at?"

"Maybe," Molly said. "Something like that."

"Was his accident not an accident? Is that what you're asking me?"

"No," Molly said. Now her mother was the one who was glaring.

"Because if you are, I can tell you. It was not intentional. It was an accident."

"Okay," Molly said.

"He didn't crash his car on purpose."

"How do you know?"

"I know because I know."

"He drove on that stretch of highway year after year, hundreds and hundreds of times. And then one night he goes off the road at full speed."

"The police think he might have dozed off," her mother said. "Fallen asleep."

"But he was always drinking coffee."

"I know, I know. Go figure."

"It doesn't make sense," Molly said. "Why?"

"Don't you think I've asked myself the same thing?" For once her mother didn't sound composed. Beneath her buoyant new hairdo, her face was twisted with confusion.

"And?" Molly asked.

"There is no *why*, Molly. There's just *is*."

Her mother cleared the dishes from the table and returned with a cup of hot water and a tea bag. "There's something I want you to think about," she said.

"Sure," Molly said. "I'll think about anything."

"Good," her mother said. "I want you to think about moving."

"Moving?" Molly said. At first Molly didn't understand what she meant. It seemed like a weird thing to say. "As opposed to standing still?"

"As opposed to staying in this house, in this city."

Her mother had never liked Buffalo. She'd come because it was where she and Molly's dad both found good jobs after college. She'd thought they'd just be passing through. Buffalo would be a short, funny line on her résumé. For her, just like for the rest of the country, it was a punch line, the city of snow and Super Bowl losers, the city of chicken wings and unemployment. It was part of the Rust Belt. Where the big ideas for urban renewal were casino gambling and a fishing tackle superstore. It was what people hoped didn't happen to their cities. It was like Siberia, a place you'd go to disappear, to be punished.

"Moving as in van," Molly said.

"Back to Milwaukee," her mother said. The house would be just one more thing to be discarded, just like her dad's clothes.

"Milwaukee," Molly said. It was where her mother grew up, where they made car trips every other summer to pay a visit.

"We would be near Grandma. A new job for me, a new school for you. It could be a fresh start. For both of us."

Molly felt too exhausted to say anything. Where would she even begin? She didn't especially want to be nearer to her grandmother. To Molly, Buffalo was no joke. For better or worse, it was home. She didn't want a fresh start. Maybe her life was messed up, but she wasn't ready to trade it for a new one.

Molly stood up. With her new haircut and hopeful offer, her mother seemed like some kind of sales agent.

"I'll definitely think about it," Molly said. She felt as if she and her mother maybe were supposed to shake hands at that point, like shady business partners contemplating some kind of greasy deal.

Later, alone in her room, Molly looked out her window and studied the blinking red light of the distant radio tower. She thought about little Caitlin next door, snug in her bed, and remembered the view from her room. Molly couldn't think of a single wish to wish. She was completely wishless.

She thought about what her mother had told her about her dad's accident. Why was she not relieved to hear that what she had feared most was not what had happened? Was a terrible explanation better than no explanation? How could her dad have fallen asleep? What was he thinking? How could he have done that to her?

Molly's life felt like one of those impossible knots she got in her sneaker laces when she was a little girl. The more she worked at it, the harder she pulled, the worse it got. She was part of a team that didn't seem to want her; annoyed with a boy who was maybe her friend, maybe just a catcher; obsessed with a crazy pitch taught to her by a father who fell asleep at the wheel; at war with her mother, who wanted her just to get over it and move on, whatever "it" was.

She looked down below, stared into the darkness of the lawn, her old playground, where, just a couple of weeks before, after her last blowout with her mother, she'd thrown that one magical knuckler. So much had happened since then. It seemed so long ago.

But even now Molly didn't want to get over baseball, and she sure didn't want to get over her dad. She didn't even want to get over her grief, that aching sadness in her chest. It connected her to him. It was a painful connection, but it was a connection just the same, and she would never willingly give that up.

Molly opened the window. There was a breeze, which felt good. She tried to imagine herself down in the yard, winding up, her dad crouched and giving her a target. She squinted into the shadows and could almost see it. The white ball, released from her hand, floating, dipping and rising in impossible waves, riding the air current like a hawk, floating, floating, floating.

16. MOLLY'S GRIP

"So Eva Schmidt's mother spilled the beans," Molly told Celia. "Told my mom all about it."

They were at Celia's house, down in the basement, a big family rec room full of interesting stuff—baskets of laundry, a drum set, a Ping-Pong table piled with boxes of old books, a stationary bike, skis and skates, a pair of crutches. Celia's parents stayed out—if they needed something, they shouted down the stairs. It was like a clubhouse, an independent nation.

Celia was sitting on a folding chair, holding her tuba, the big mouthpiece covering her lips. She conveyed her sympathetic disgust by shaking her head slowly back and forth.

"Busted," Molly said. She was standing with her back to Celia. She brought her hands together at her waist and looked over her shoulder at her. In Molly's hand was a rolled-up pair of sweat socks. She was practicing pitching from the stretch position, going through the motions so they would become automatic, second nature. With runners on base, she couldn't use the full windup she knew best—if she did, they'd steal. Instead, she had to use this modified motion, including a pause, during which she was supposed to look at the runners, fix them with a stare. If a runner strayed too far from the base, she was supposed to throw over and pick him off.

"She was going to find out sooner or later," Celia said.

"I know," Molly said. "But still."

Celia squinted at the music on the stand in front of her—she needed glasses but was in denial about it—and blew a funky-sounding bass line. Molly stepped forward and tossed the sock-ball across the room. She followed through just as she would have for real.

The team's first game was just a week away. It seemed impossible that she would ever be ready. It was one thing to practice, one thing to do it right in Celia's basement or in a drill with no one watching, when you had the chance to do it over if you messed up. It was something else entirely to do it when it counted, against kids you didn't know, on the varsity field, in front of a crowd.

"Does she know about Lonnie?" Celia asked.

"Know what about Lonnie?" Molly said. "What is there to know about Lonnie?" There'd been no more visits to her house. But he always caught her at practice. They had a few awkward telephone conversations. He waited for her after practice sometimes, and they talked, a little. "*I don't know about Lonnie,*" Molly said.

After the last practice he had called her to see if she was okay. Molly had been a little short with him, she wasn't sure why. He seemed concerned, but maybe not concerned enough. Or not concerned in the right way. Or something. The thing about Lonnie was that on the phone he was not a real live wire. He was no chatterbox, that was for sure. All those words written across the back of his hand, but put him on the phone and not that many came out of his mouth. Plus, in the background there was always some unhappy static, some kind of miserable Muzak—the grinding of what sounded like his mother complaining, droning on unpleasantly about something. It was not as if Molly was looking to import more unhappiness into her life at this particular point.

"What's the matter?" Celia asked. "You two have a tiff? Are you breaking up?"

Molly went through the motions of her stretch windup again. Brought her hands together. This time she looked back over her right shoulder, at an imaginary runner leading off second base.

"I'm not sure we were ever together," Molly said. "So how could we break up?"

"Why is your hand like that?" Celia said.

"Like what?"

Celia pointed. "All weird and clawlike, all crumpled up."

Molly had to laugh. "That's my grip," she said. "For the knuckleball." Even if it was only a rolled-up pair of socks, that was how she held it. That much at least had become automatic. "Remember? My secret weapon?"

For the next twenty minutes or so, each of them kept practicing. Celia blew her horn, the same basic rhythm with some Jamaican-flavored variations. If anyone could play reggae tuba, it would be Celia. Molly kept working from the stretch, checking imaginary runners on the bases, holding them close.

They were together, but they didn't speak. For that time, Molly felt as almost-happy as she had in a long time, at peace even. She liked being with Celia, she liked the music, she liked going through the pitching movements without having to think, she liked not talking. Maybe her trouble with Lonnie wasn't too few words, maybe it was the need for words in the first place.

The next afternoon Molly threw an inning in a practice game. Her knuckleball was maddeningly inconsistent. It started out fine, and she got a couple of quick outs. But then it turned into a wild, willful child. It wouldn't listen to her. She walked the bases full.

Lonnie, who'd been brought into the scrimmage along with Molly, came out for a conference. He was breathing hard but didn't seem upset. He raised his mask and shrugged. If her knuckleball was going berserk, he wasn't going to hold it against her.

"I know," Molly said.

"Okay," Lonnie said.

He was a weird kid, but he had a good heart, and Molly couldn't stay mad at him for long.

With runners on base, at least Molly felt comfortable working from a stretch. All that practice in Celia's basement must have paid off. She checked the runners, at third, second, and first. She noticed that the runner leading off first, Eli Krause, had wandered pretty far from the base and didn't seem to be paying all that much attention to her. Everett Sheets, the first baseman, had sneaked in behind him and was flapping his mitt. He wanted Molly to throw it over.

She took a breath, then, just as she'd been coached, pivoted hard toward first and threw to Everett. It was a strong move, except that what Molly threw to Everett was a knuckleball. Molly watched, horrified, as the spinless ball started shoulder high, then dove. Somehow, though, Everett snagged it in his mitt and applied the tag to Eli, who didn't even slide back into the base—he'd been caught flat-footed. Molly heard someone on the bench cackling with delight— it sounded like Coach V—and just like that, Molly was out of the inning.

At the end of practice Morales called the team together. Coach V, who'd disappeared a few minutes earlier, returned carrying a big cardboard box.

"Take a seat," Morales said.

In the box were the team jerseys and caps. Morales had a system for distributing them. It was a little ritual, like a graduation. He asked the players to take a seat in front of him on the grass. Molly settled on one knee near the back, next to Lonnie, who was still wearing his shin guards. One by one, Morales called their names. Each player stood and stepped forward, took a jersey from Morales and a cap from Coach V.

There was nothing special about the uniforms. They were blue double-knit jerseys with white lettering, blue caps with black brims. But still, there was something about them. To Molly, and any other true fan like her dad, a team uniform—the Yankees' pinstripes, for example—could trigger a whole range of memories and emotions. How a player wore his uniform could tell you something about him. Some were baggy, unbuttoned, and dusty. Some were trim and tucked. You could wear it like a gangster, a hotdog, an old-fashioned dirt eater, a bland company man. But no matter what, the uniform, however you styled it, showed your membership, connected you with something. Gave you something to represent. Somebody wore those colors before, and someone would wear them afterward.

Molly watched as Morales called her teammates forward one by one and handed them their jerseys. They didn't shake hands, but there was something sort of congratulatory about it. Morales held each jersey up in front of the player, eyeballing them for size, Molly supposed, but there was a kind of formality about it. Desmond, Lloyd, Ian, James, Everett, Lonnie—each took a shirt from Morales and moved down the line to receive a cap from Coach V. The idea seemed to be that a uniform was something they'd earned, that wearing the uniform meant something.

Molly was among the last to be called up. She stood and approached Morales, who showed her the front, then the back. There was a big white 49, the traditional knuckleballer's number. "Thank you," Molly said, and felt a little choked up. When Coach V handed her a cap, he may or may not have winked at her. His face was so wrinkled and twitchy, it was impossible to tell whether it was a sign or just a tic.

* * *

That night after dinner, Molly went into the bathroom upstairs and tried on her uniform. She pulled the jersey over the white turtleneck she had on and tugged at the shoulders. It fit okay. A little roomy, which was fine. She studied the lettering reversed in the mirror. MCKINLEY. Her father used to think it was funny that her school was named after an obscure president who came to Buffalo a hundred years ago and was assassinated by a crazy man. Her mother thought it was sick.

Molly pulled her hair back and put the cap on her head. She gently curved the bill. She looked into the mirror and made the face she showed to batters, the face she checked runners with. Would anyone take her seriously? Did she look like a pitcher or a poser?

Molly took a step back. She tugged on the brim of her cap and pretended to look in for a sign from her catcher. In the mirror she seemed to glimpse, just for an instant, not herself, not her current anxiety-ridden self, but the little girl she used to be, the little girl in the home movie, pitching to her dad on a sunny day without a care in the world. That little girl was full of spit and vinegar, that little girl was fearless and unself-conscious. She didn't need to read a book in order to learn how to be in the moment. That little girl didn't care what she looked like when she threw the ball. She just did it, ferociously.

Out in the hall, Molly's mother was putting away laundry in the linen closet. Molly could hear the creak of the door and her mother's exhaling in an exhausted, sad sort of way. It was what middle age sounded like. All day on the phone at work, her mother was brisk and full of can-do energy, but at night, when she thought no one was listening, she sounded defeated.

On impulse, Molly opened the door and stepped out.

"So what do you think?" she asked. She spun around and struck a goofy pose, arms crossed across her chest.

Her mother stepped forward and tugged gently at the hem of the jersey, felt the double-knit fabric. If it had been a prom dress, her mother would have known perfectly how to respond. But because this was a baseball uniform, she seemed perplexed. There was no lace, nothing that gathered or plunged.

"Well?" Molly said.

Molly could tell that her mother was trying very hard not to say the wrong thing. "It's very striking," her mother said at last. She seemed so cautious, nervous even. She seemed scared that Molly might go off. Molly felt sorry for all her testiness in the past. She didn't like thinking that she'd become an emotional terrorist, always on the verge of detonating.

"Is it *me*? Molly asked. She wanted to keep it light, the way she would with Celia. "Do I look fabulous?"

"Oh yes," her mother said. "It is you. It is so you."

"You think?"

"Think?" her mother said. "I *know*. Nothing could be more you."

17. SIGNS

*D*uring practice that week, the team worked on the finer points of playing the field—defending against the bunt, executing cutoffs. Molly learned that if she gave up a big hit, she couldn't just stand on the mound and kick the rubber in disgust. There was no time to be angry with herself. She had to back up third base.

Every day Molly learned how much more there was to baseball than what the camera showed on television. With a runner on first base, it was the pitcher's responsibility to talk to the shortstop and second baseman, letting them know who should cover second. When a ball was hit into the air, Molly was supposed to point at it so that her fielders could pick it up. And if the first and third basemen were both charging a bunt, it was Molly's job to call out who should take it and where to throw it. Shouting didn't come naturally to Molly, but Morales teased her into it. He cupped his ear like an old, hard-of-hearing man. "Did someone say something?" Before long, Molly was hollering out instructions to her infielders loud and clear. She stopped worrying about sounding ladylike and concentrated on being heard.

Morales was gentle with physical errors. They were unavoidable, part of the game. What really bugged him were examples of what he called a failure to communicate. Two outfielders running into each other because neither called for the ball, that sort of thing. "You gotta talk to each other," he told them over and over again.

At the last practice before their game Morales sat them on the bench and taught them a simple set of signs they'd use when the team was up to bat. If he touched his belt buckle, that was the indicator: What followed then was the real sign, the rest was gibberish. A touch of the forearm meant steal, the bill of his cap was bunt.

Molly had always liked to watch the third-base coaches in big league games, all their twitchy antics, their elaborate coded messages, all that clapping, pointing, wiping. It was comical, but beyond the goofy theatrics, the whole idea fascinated her: an entire system of wordless communication. She loved the beautiful, perfect clarity of it. A touch of the forearm meant steal. Nothing more, nothing less. There was no chance to be misunderstood. There was no need to puzzle over what it meant.

It occurred to Molly that maybe she and her mother

ought to try communicating using signs. It was an appealing fantasy. The two of them sitting across from each other at dinner, silent, just touching their elbows, going to their belt buckles, tugging their earlobes. It would make for a funny skit. But what if you wanted to convey something more complicated than "bunt" or "steal"? That was the trouble. "I love you and all that, but right now everything about you bothers me." What would be the sign for something like that? Or how about this: "Please don't make me move to Milwaukee." Half the time Molly had no idea what she wanted to get across. No signs could help with that.

During that last practice, it occurred to Molly that in this country of baseball, she was still a kind of alien. Not a tourist. She was learning the customs, could speak the language well enough to get by. But she still didn't quite fit in. Someone like Ben Malone was native born, fluent. He belonged so naturally, he didn't even know it. He took it for granted, he didn't have to think about it. He had no idea how much energy it took to be as ever-vigilant as Molly had to be on the field, always watching herself, always planning her next move, rehearsing, calculating.

Molly watched enviously as Ben walked along the bench, nonchalantly untucking the shirttails of teammates as he passed by. Without asking permission, he would reach casually into a teammate's bag of sunflower seeds and help himself to a big handful. He knew he was entitled. It was only partly a guy thing.

Molly wasn't the only one. Lonnie was likewise peripheral. Put him in a lineup with Ben Malone and Mario Coppola and play a quick round of One of These Things Just Doesn't Belong. Lonnie would get chosen every single time. It was hard to say why, tough to put into words just what it was about him. Something. The way he wore his cap, maybe. His humming. Possibly the fact that his mitt was covered with pictograms. Impossible to define precisely, but real.

In an entirely different way, for completely different reasons, Desmond Davis and James Castle inhabited the margins, too. They were the only African American kids on the team, among the few in a mostly white school. Of course, they were never explicitly excluded from anything. Molly never witnessed anything that could be considered prejudice. Never any name-calling, no meanness. Just the opposite. Molly sensed everyone wanted to show how not-prejudiced they were. It reminded Molly a little of how she had been treated after her dad's funeral, with a kind of studied, almost scripted niceness. To all appearances it was just right, but it didn't *feel* real.

There seemed to be invisible barriers, unspoken rules. At school Desmond and James ate lunch together, and at practice they almost always played catch together. They had private, quiet conversations on the bench that halted if you got too near. They even had their own handshake. It was an elaborate one, with many steps. It involved both the front and back of the hand, some knuckle, high and low slaps, some finger snapping. They could do it superfast. They weren't showy about it, but Molly saw them do it a couple of times and, once again, couldn't help but feel like an envious outsider.

* * *

The night before the game, Molly couldn't sleep. She tossed and she turned. She tried to think of the most sleep-inducing topic she could. It was the endless memorization of science, her least favorite subject. She tried, instead of counting sheep, listing the parts of the cell she was going to be quizzed on later in the week. Endoplasmic reticulum. Golgi bodies and lysosomes. Plasma cell membrane. Ribosomes. She had this stuff down cold. She could label a cell diagram with her eyes closed, she could spell "mitochondria" backward and forward.

These mental gymnastics weren't making her the least bit drowsy. Finally she gave up and got out of bed. She picked up the ball lying on her desk. As always, it felt good in her hand. The thing was, the ball didn't care. That's what she loved about it. It was completely indifferent, without prejudice. The ball didn't care if you were a girl or a boy. Skinny or fat, rich or poor, black or white, cool or uncool, happy or sad, smart and funny or awkward and shy, if you were charming and had a way with words and a winning smile—didn't matter. The ball didn't care.

She looked out the window and saw the flickering glow of a television next door in the Rybaks' house. It was one A.M. Face it: Nobody watched television at this hour because of the high-quality programming. Did Mr. Rybak have insomnia? Mrs. Rybak? They didn't seem like the sleepless types. What could possibly be keeping them awake at this hour? Molly had assumed that their happy, wholesome, well-regulated lives excluded all confusion, doubt, middle-of-the-night dread. So maybe not. Maybe the walls of even the nicest, most carefully constructed homes were semipermeable membranes. Siding, double-pane windows, caulk—it didn't matter; sorrow and confusion were going to leak through from time to time.

There was a phrase Molly had heard her dad use more than once: Dark night of the soul. She hadn't understood it at the time, but the words stuck with her. They must have scared her a little. So this was probably it. Her dark night. It sounded worse than it was. It wasn't so bad.

Molly stepped away from the window and toed an imaginary rubber. She knew she looked ridiculous, standing in her bedroom wearing plaid flannel pajama pants and a Bills T-shirt, in the middle of the night, getting ready to pitch. But no one was watching. It was her bedroom, her dark night of the soul; she could do whatever she pleased. She gripped the ball for a knuckler, rocked into her windup, and coming over the top the way Morales had coached her, went through the motion of delivering a pitch home.

Her arm felt good.

18. GAME DAY

*W*hen she took her seat next to Lonnie in English class the next morning, Molly noticed that his hand had been injured. His thumb was swollen, purplish, painful-looking.

"Hey," she said, and pointed. "What happened?"

"Dunno," Lonnie said. He shrugged. Put a look on his face that was supposed to express bewilderment. He was a terrible liar, which was something Molly liked about him. She knew exactly how he must have hurt himself. One of her wild pitches must have ricocheted off his mitt and caught his bare hand. It happened a lot.

She'd done it to him. Being her personal catcher was no treat. There was a good reason why even big league catchers hated catching knuckleballers. Nobody wanted to go through that misery, endure all the sprains and bruises. Who wanted to get beat up?

Molly didn't like to think she was capable of injuring someone else. Her mother, her father, the jerkhead boys on the team—they'd injured *her*, she'd been the victim. That was how she thought of herself, as innocent. But clearly, she could dish out some hurt, too. The evidence was right in front of her. Lonnie's knuckles looked scraped and raw, too, and there were some yellowish bruises on his forearm. She was going to have to readjust her thinking about herself.

"Does it hurt?" Molly asked.

"Not a bit," Lonnie said. Which had to be another lie. It hurt just to look at his hand.

Molly felt terrible that she'd done it to him. On the other hand, she couldn't help but think that bruising Lonnie made for a weird kind of intimacy between them. You could kiss someone hard enough to put a bruise on them. It was a physical connection. She'd left her mark on him.

During homeroom, as part of the morning announcements, the details of the game that afternoon were broadcast by Vice Principal Niedermeyer. Normally, announcements were made by two students, but this week's pair apparently had been fired the day before for reading the announcements in crazy accents. Something like that was too funny to be tolerated. In the vice principal's voice, even a baseball game—four o'clock start, home field, first game of the year, come and support the team—sounded ominous somehow. When he spoke, everything sounded ominous. He had a voice that made you want to duck and cover.

The vice principal referred to the team as "the boys'

baseball team." Molly wouldn't have thought about it one way or another, but that phrase, presumably, and Molly's presence in the room, seemed to evoke a reaction from some girls in the back. There was some laughter, some tittering and pointed looks. Molly wasn't paranoid, but she knew when she was being talked about.

The girls were an A-list clique. Celia called them The Mindys, though only one of them was actually named Mindy, Mindy Banks. There was also a Jodi, a Lindsay, a Hailey, and an April. When Celia called them that, The Mindys, it always sounded to Molly like the name of a band. They didn't actually play anything, but here, in this little world, they were stars, minor celebrities. Skinny and glamorous. Lots of eye makeup. Kids gossiped about them, noticed what they wore. Boys whose names they probably didn't even know had crushes on them. They were always well turned out, always on. In their own way they were performance artists.

"When I said I was going out for baseball," Molly said, "you told me that I was Amelia Earhart. I was a pioneer, you said. You remember that?"

Celia nodded. "Sure," she said. "I remember that."

"So how come they don't seem to think so?"

"Just wait," Celia said. "It takes time. At first the other girls didn't know Amelia Earhart was Amelia Earhart. Know what I mean?"

Molly didn't, in fact, know what she meant, but she said she did, which was what she often did when faced with this sort of Celia-ism. It was just easier. "Of course," Molly said. "It takes time."

* * *

On her way to fifth period Molly passed Morales in the hall. He was dressed as a mild-mannered social studies teacher, pushing an overhead projector on a rolling cart, but he was apparently thinking about the game.

"How's the arm?" he asked.

"Dandy," Molly said. Dandy? What a weird thing to have come out of her mouth! She had never used the word in her life. Who said that? What did it even mean?

But Morales seemed unfazed. "Good," he said. "We may need you."

"Sure," Molly said. Though at first it didn't register—what he meant, who the "we" was who might need her.

Alone, in a far corner of the girls' locker room, Molly changed into her uniform. She could hear, not see, the track team getting ready for practice, the happy hum of their talk, the squeak of their sneakers.

Always self-conscious about dressing and undressing, Molly in a way was a little glad to be an exile in the locker room, grateful for the privacy. Sometimes, entering and exiting the practice field alone through the girls' door while the boys crowded through theirs in a pack, she felt a little special. But this afternoon she just felt lonely. She missed Tess and Ruth. Who was playing third base these days? She even missed Lu Baxter. Was she still dancing in the outfield? Working on any new routines? If Molly weren't alone, if she had someone to joke with, maybe she wouldn't feel so nervous now.

Molly smoothed the front of her jersey, made sure that her socks were straight. Her black uniform pants were neither baggy nor tight—they were comfortable, just right. She thought of her mother giving her uniform a thumbs-up. Molly knew that from her mother's perspective, she'd always been insufficiently interested in style. They hadn't shared too many chummy shopping sprees—when they bought Molly's clothes, it was often testy, a battle of wills. For her mother not to offer some kind of full-blown fashion critique, that was something. At breakfast that morning Molly had mentioned the game to her, very low-key, just sort of FYI, and her mother didn't freak—she just kept blowing on her coffee and said good luck, which seemed to Molly just right.

Molly checked the wall clock—in three minutes she was supposed to be on the field for warm-ups. There was a full-length mirror near the door leading to the field, and Molly stopped to take one last look at herself. She didn't want to look fashionable, just professional, and Molly, giving herself as objective a once-over as she could, figured she passed—she looked like a ballplayer.

She was about to take the field for her first game, uniformed, wearing her cap the way she always did in the backyard, brim slightly curved, pulled low over her eyes to make herself look fierce. At that moment, naturally, she thought of her dad.

You look good, Molly. It's a dandy uniform.

That was your word! I should have known.

How you feeling? You look a little pale.

I'm nervous, Dad. I don't want to be Amelia Earhart. Look what happened to her!

You don't have to be anyone but you. Just be Molly Williams.

Molly Williams is scared.

Scared of what?

I don't know. What if I make a horrible error? What if I make a royal fool of myself?

What if?

What if I let the team down? I let you down?

You've got nothing to prove, Molly. You don't have to cheer me up. I'm proud of you. Do your best. Have some fun.

Fun? Fun?

Molly looked at the clock—she was a minute late. She grabbed her glove and, cleats clicking across the locker-room floor, headed out toward the field.

19. GIMME SOME

*M*olly jogged out and joined her teammates, who were just lining up in right field to start stretching. The varsity field had been fenced off all spring, KEEP OUT signs posted every ten feet or so. Now, in May, it was in terrific shape. The infield dirt was smooth, the mound raked, the foul lines and batter's box neatly chalked. The grass was thick and green. After so many practices on their bumpy, dandelion-filled practice field, this was something else. Molly almost felt guilty for being on the field at all, half expecting someone to holler at her to get off.

Dressed in their brand-new unis and let loose on the well-manicured field, everyone seemed a little formal, self-conscious and cautious, like kids dressed up in their Sunday best. Coach V must have sensed how they felt. "It's okay to get dirty," he said, walking among them while they got down to stretch. "You won't get in trouble. Grass stains are good. You want your parents to know you played."

They went through the familiar routine, second nature now after performing it practice after practice, week after week. Molly stretched and tried, unsuccessfully, to empty her mind. She focused on her breathing. But despite her best effort to embrace the stillness of her inner depths and all that, her mind was full. It was overflowing.

She would never be a Zen master. She didn't have a single inner voice, she had a chorus of voices, all of them shouting questions, like reporters at a news conference. She wondered if the other team was going to harass her about being a girl. She worried that she wasn't going to get into the game; she worried that she *was* going to get into the game. There was a breeze blowing in from center field—would it help or hurt her knuckleball?

While they were running, a bus pulled into the parking lot. The doors opened and a line of boys in red jerseys filed off. Several men came last, a whole committee of coaches in matching shirts, carrying big canvas bags of gear, buckets full of baseballs, first-aid tackle boxes. Molly kept running, but of course, just like the rest of her teammates, she was checking them out.

The team came from Sheridan, a more distant, wealthier suburb, which called itself a village. The streets there all had names like Fawn Trail and Deer Run. Judging from a street map, you might think it was a wildlife preserve. The players had their names sewn across the backs of the jerseys, just like the pros. To Molly some of the Sheridan boys looked physically intimidating—taller, more muscled up. One kid had a mustache. A big batter has a big strike zone, Molly's dad liked to point out, which was easy to say when you were sitting on the couch.

Molly played catch as she usually did with Lonnie. His hand didn't seem to be bothering him. He looked good in his uniform. Unlike the thing he wore at practices, his uniform cap seemed to fit and sat relatively straight on his head. Underneath, his hair was under control, sort of. He looked like a real ballplayer.

On the first-base side of the field, people were filling in the wooden bleachers; some were beginning to settle in to watch the game from along the right-field line. Mom and dad and grandparent types were unfolding chairs, spreading blankets, setting up the toddlers with coloring books.

Lonnie threw one ball over Molly's head, and the next one was in the dirt. Molly's return throw bounced off the heel of his glove. What was up with him? All of a sudden he couldn't play catch?

Lonnie wasn't paying attention, that was the problem. His head was turning again and again to the sidelines—he was checking out the fans. Molly pretended to stretch her trunk and, as subtly as she could, turned to have a look herself.

There was one man Lonnie was completely focused on. It was easy to pick him out. He was wearing a pink polo shirt, holding a baby on his chest in a Snugli. Molly knew it had to be Lonnie's dad. He looked like the poster boy for midlife crisis. Next to him there was a tan, blond woman with sunglasses perched on her head. Molly recognized them immediately from Lonnie's description. They were the new, improved family.

Part of Molly felt jealous of Lonnie, just for an instant, that he had a dad at the game at all, even a pink-shirted one. It was a kind of spasm—quick, involuntary, and painful. But it passed. It passed as soon as she glanced back at Lonnie and saw how he looked. He didn't look scared, he didn't look upset. He looked abandoned—and forlorn, that was the word. He looked as sad and as hopeless as the word sounded. Painfully aware that there was nothing he could do, not today, not ever, to measure up, to win the day. In baseball lingo, he'd been mathematically eliminated, and he knew it. Lonnie looked as if he wished he were somewhere else, as if he wished he were someone else.

Over the past several weeks, Lonnie had revealed bits and pieces about his dad, very cautiously, a detail or two here, a story there. He'd taken to waiting for Molly after practice, not always, but usually. She'd step out of the girls' locker room and find him there on the sidewalk, sitting on his bike, spinning a pedal, loitering. She was always glad to see him. They lived in the same general direction, so they walked along together for a few blocks, Lonnie pushing his old bike alongside Molly on the sidewalk, until they parted ways at Molly's corner. They made small talk, about school, about practice. Or they just went along in silence. Occasionally Lonnie would volunteer something about his family situation, his dad in the suburbs and his new half sister. Molly just listened. She never pressed for more. Always

Lonnie framed things in a good light. He'd seen baby Zoey only a few times, but he obviously adored her. Still, Molly got the picture. Lonnie's father was a guy who fulfilled his court-ordered visitation to the letter of the law, never a day more, hardly a minute more. He had a wallet containing a whole album of Zoeys and not a single Lonnie. The new wife called Lonnie "my husband's son."

Molly understood why Lonnie looked so stricken. She had probably never cared more for him than she did at that moment. She wanted to protect him, to be a fierce advocate for him. She felt like slapping his father's self-satisfied face, she felt like kicking dirt on his wicked step-mother. But what good would that do?

"Okay," Molly shouted to Lonnie. "I'm warm," which is what you say when you're through playing catch. Lonnie looked relieved and grateful. Together they jogged off the field and into the dugout.

A dugout was one of the things Molly had always envied about boys' baseball. The girls' teams, for some reason, always sat on benches, exposed. A dugout was private, half underground—you stepped down into it. It felt protected, like a bomb shelter, and exclusive, like a clubhouse, some-place you'd need to know a secret password to enter.

Morales had posted the starting lineup and batting order on the dugout wall:

1. Eli Krause 2B
2. James Castle CF
3. Desmond Davis P
4. Lloyd Coleman SS

5. Mario Coppola 3B
6. Everett Sheets 1B
7. Ryan Vogel RF
8. Ian Meriwether LF
9. Ben Malone C

Molly and Lonnie looked it over and then sat down side by side on the bench in silence. Molly couldn't think of anything to say. She was starting to feel angry with herself now, her amazing non-way with words, when she heard Lonnie clear his throat. Then he let loose a stream of spit in the direction of the field. Molly had never seen Lonnie spit before—he wasn't the spitting type. But this was a surprisingly strong effort, well executed, with respectable distance. It landed in the dirt outside the dugout. It was a brave gesture, it seemed to Molly, much more to the point than anything she could have said.

"Okay," Lonnie said, mostly to himself. It was as if he had expelled something poisonous and was feeling better already. He pounded his fist into his mitt a couple of times. The other team was taking the field for infield practice. Mustache Boy was jogging over to take first base. He kicked the bag. There was something about him Molly just didn't like. His attitude, which was something like ownership, or entitlement. First base was his, he seemed to think—the field, the game, it was all his. Molly cleared her throat and got ready for her first spit of the season.

Five minutes before game time, Coach Morales took Everett Sheets and Eli Krause, the tall and the short of it, to home plate to meet with the umpire and the Sheridan coach and captains. Molly watched them, sitting by herself now in the corner of the dugout. Lonnie was down at the other end of the bench, filling up a cup with water from the team's plastic cooler. Desmond Davis and James Castle were standing just a few feet away from Molly, flexing and stretching, getting ready to take the field.

"Gimme some," Desmond said to James, and they launched into their handshake. There seemed to be some new flourishes, a few more fancy touches at the end that made Molly smile. She envied their style, their private language of friendship.

Desmond noticed that Molly had been watching. He paused for just a beat, as if deciding something, then spoke. "Molly," he said.

She was afraid that she'd invaded their space, intruded upon a private ritual that was none of her business. She was just about to apologize, but Desmond interrupted her. "Come on," he said. "I'll show you how it's done."

Desmond broke it down for her, step by step, while James looked on, grinning. Two times through and she had it down. Slap, slap, up and down, knuckle and elbow, with a near miss and a wiggle at the end. She'd never say so, but it was just a hipper version of patty-cake, rhythmic and percussive, a little combative but still friendly. She and Desmond ran through it once more, full speed, and neither missed a beat.

Watching them, James cracked up. Molly had never seen him so animated. "Okay, girl," James said. "One more time. Gimme some."

20. KEEPING SCORE

*M*olly was sitting next to Coach V on the bench, watching the game and watching V keep score. It was the bottom of the fifth. Morales was busy coaching third base, giving signs to the batter and shouting instructions to the base runners, so it was up to V to record what happened in the official scorebook.

Ian Meriwether took ball four, tossed his bat aside, and jogged down to first base. Coach V wrote a "w" for walk in the little square reserved for Ian and the fifth inning and drew a line, showing he'd advanced to first.

Coach V used the same basic system of scorekeeping Molly had learned from her dad. V's method did have its

145

own peculiarities, some eccentric variations. He kept track of every single pitch, for one thing, something her dad never did—balls, strikes, even foul balls—with tiny antlike marks. Plus he talked while he scored, kept up a little private commentary.

When Ben Malone took a called third strike at the knees, V made a large K in his box. No one had ever told Molly why K was the symbol of a strikeout, not S or SO, but she understood it was more fitting somehow, more dramatic, even brutal. Coach drew this K backward to show that Ben's strikeout was looking rather than swinging. "What can you do with a pitch like that?" he asked sadly.

Molly understood that keeping score was a kind of storytelling, an almost magical translation of loud and dusty events in the world—a stolen base, an around-the-horn double play, a triple—into pencil marks, a kind of secret code, numbers and lines and shapes, like cuneiform or hieroglyphics, the handiwork of some ancient scribe.

In Coach V's book, Molly could read the story of the game so far. Not just the score, McKinley 3, Sheridan 2, but also how the runs came about. In the first inning, the first three McKinley batters—Eli, James, and Desmond—had gotten on base, an infield single and two walks. What the scorebook didn't show, but what Molly remembered, was how nervous the Sheridan pitcher had looked, or what a joyful scene it was when Lloyd Coleman cleared the bases with a double—whistles and cheers from the grandstand, whoops and high fives in the dugout.

Back then, in the first inning, it looked easy. The game seemed like it was going to be a blowout. What's so hard about this game? That's what it felt like. But Molly knew baseball didn't work that way. You're cruising along one minute, feeling like you can do no wrong. Life is good, all's right with the world. And then all of sudden, for no apparent reason, things change.

Now the Sheridan pitcher—Jarvis, the back of his shirt said—had regained his composure. He'd shut McKinley down since the first inning, while his team got back two of the runs. Molly watched him work on the mound. Not as a fan. And even though he was a nice-enough-looking boy, not that way either. She watched as a fellow practitioner, another member of the club. Coach Morales would approve of his mechanics. He came hard over the top and always followed through. He had good stuff—a fastball with some movement, and a tantalizing slow curve. He threw two of those curves for strikes to Eli Krause, who watched both of them with a look of amazement on his face.

Behind in the count 0-2, Eli swung and missed a pitch almost over his head. Coach V made another K in the book. Molly meanwhile was fantasizing about a scoring system not for baseball but for life. If she said something stupid, forgot to bring home her science book—those would be errors. If her mother came through for her about a third of the time— that sounded about right—her batting average would be .333. Back when her locker had been defaced and Lonnie came along and rescued her, he could have been credited with a save.

Would a system like that be a brilliant invention? Or would it be a nightmare? James Castle made the third out by popping up to the second baseman, and V recorded it in his book. "No runs, no hits, no errors," he muttered. "One man left on base."

Molly was grateful in fact that her every error off the field had not been counted and tabulated and published in the Sunday paper. In everyday language, if you said someone was keeping score, it meant they carried a grudge. To imagine V making note of all her mistakes, her fumbles and whiffs, writing them down for posterity—it gave her the willies. Maybe forgetfulness could be a gift, a kind of blessing.

Between innings, Molly grabbed her glove and a ball and warmed up Ryan Vogel, the right fielder. In band he used to bug her, but he was okay as a teammate. He wasn't obnoxious on the field. Playing catch with him was something she didn't mind doing. It needed to be done, for one thing. The infielders threw the ball around among themselves, the center fielder played catch with the left fielder, and the right fielder was the odd man out. So it was a way for her to be a team player, to contribute something even though she wasn't in the game. (For the first couple of innings, she'd been lining up the bats and batting helmets but stopped when it occurred to her that it was too domestic—let the boys tidy up after themselves.) She liked to stay loose, too. Among the half dozen throws she exchanged with Ryan, she mixed in one knuckleball, which floated beautifully. But it made Ryan complain.

"Hey," he said. "Knock it off."

Molly didn't want to get fired as right fielder warmer-upper, so she resolved to refrain, to control her urge to knuckle.

Jogging back to the dugout, Molly once again scanned the bleachers, the sidelines, the cars in the lot angled toward the field. Between the second and third innings, she'd spotted Celia. She had her current needlework project on her lap, a vest—stitchery was her latest mania—but she set her needle and thread down long enough to give Molly an enthusiastic wave. And behind Celia were Tess Warren and Ruth Schwab, her old softball teammates. If they'd been hurt by her defection to the boys' team, Molly was glad they were over it. It was good of them to come out.

Now she was looking for her mom. Molly was certain she had told her at breakfast the right time and the right place. But Molly couldn't find her, and she was surprised that she was so disappointed. She had told herself it didn't matter, one way or another, she didn't care. Whatever. But she did care. What had Celia told her? It's okay to want something.

The next inning, the top of the sixth, Desmond got the first Sheridan batter quickly, a ground out to Lloyd Coleman at shortstop. But then he got into trouble. He walked the next batter on four pitches, none of them all that close.

"He's running out of gas," Coach V said.

Desmond had pitched a fine game. He was not stylish at all. He pretty much just stepped and threw, but with some real sizzle. Molly admired his confidence and eagerness to compete. Desmond always seemed impatient to get the ball and throw it again. But now he was slowing down, kicking the dirt around the pitcher's rubber, taking a few deep, heaving breaths.

Desmond threw three more balls to the next batter, and

all of a sudden Coach Morales was shouting her name. "Molly! Molly Williams!"

For a split second, hearing her name shouted like that, Molly thought she was in trouble. She jumped up from the bench so Morales could see her and raised her hand.

"You and Lonnie," he said. "I want you to warm up." Then he jogged out onto the field to have a chat with Desmond.

Molly grabbed her glove. Lonnie was standing in front of her, a ball and mitt and mask in hand. He looked stiff. *Reporting for duty*, that was his posture.

"How about we play some catch?" Molly said.

Lonnie looked blank. It was almost as if Molly had said, How about we rob a bank? How about we jump off a bridge?

"Sure," Lonnie said at last, a little grimly. "Sure."

Lonnie and Molly arranged themselves sixty feet apart. They didn't need to measure—by now, Molly just knew. She threw easily at first, not winding up, just tossing the ball, and then Lonnie got down into his catcher's squat and Molly started to pitch. At first she threw fastballs, hers not being all that fast, but she threw them over the plate, which was good. Even if her knuckleball was knuckling like crazy, it was smart to mix it up a little.

While she threw with Lonnie, Molly stole some glances over her shoulder to see what was happening on the field. After he'd spoken with Coach Morales, Desmond had settled down and thrown some strikes. With a full count, he got the Sheridan batter out on a weak pop-up to Eli at second base. But he got behind the next batter and walked him, too. Now there were runners on first and second, two outs. Molly could see Coach Morales standing with his foot on the top step of the dugout. He looked like he was trying to decide whether or not to go out and get Desmond.

Molly signaled to Lonnie with a flip of her glove that she was ready to start throwing knucklers. Her first one was a horror. The pitch spun, which was bad: It was a knuckleball that didn't knuckle. A pitch like that was what the boys on the team called a "meatball"—big and juicy and easy to hit.

Lonnie caught the ball, stood, and started walking toward her. Molly felt irritated. She had thrown one bad warm-up pitch, and now Lonnie House was going to give her a talking-to?

"I know, I know," Molly said. "I threw a lousy pitch. I'm warming up. Give me a break." She waved him back, but he kept coming toward her.

"Not that," he said. "Look." And pointed to the field. Coach Morales was standing on the mound with Desmond and Ben Malone. They were all staring at her and Lonnie. "He wants us," Lonnie said just as Morales gestured at them. There was no mistaking what he wanted. He pointed at them twice—you, and you—and waved them toward the mound.

"Looks like this is it," Molly said.

"Gulp," Lonnie said.

When Molly arrived on the mound, Morales had his arm on Desmond's shoulder and was speaking to him quietly. Desmond was breathing hard. He looked exhausted and frustrated.

"Hi," Morales said to Molly, which seemed like a funny thing to say under the circumstances.

"Hi," Molly said. She couldn't help but smile a little, nervous as she was. Molly had thought meeting in the school cafeteria was strange! Talking on the mound was strange to the tenth power. There was a Sheridan player loitering around second base, another one at first, touching his toes. The umpire was kneeling behind home plate, tying his shoe. From a distance, he'd looked like an old pro, but up close, Molly could see that he was maybe twenty, tops, a college kid probably.

It was one thing to watch a game from the dugout, another thing altogether to stand in the middle of things. Molly felt as if she'd walked onto the set of a movie in the middle of a shoot. Things were in full swing, everyone seemed to know their parts—everyone but her.

There was some time to kill while Lonnie was in the dugout strapping on his catcher's gear. Morales had motioned Ian in from left field and was sending Desmond out to replace him. But before he left, Desmond held out his hand. "Gimme some," he said, and they performed a subdued, slightly abbreviated version of the handshake.

Finally, Lonnie came jogging out to the mound, the buckles of his shin guards jingling. "How do you feel?" Morales asked Molly.

"I feel good," Molly said, which, true or not, she knew was the right answer.

"Good," Morales said. "You have runners on first and second, so you need to work from the stretch. You got two outs. Throw strikes and get us the last one."

Molly nodded, and Morales headed back to the dugout. Lonnie pulled his mask down, turned, and trotted to his position behind home plate.

And now, for the first time, Molly was on the mound, all alone. She thought about all her make-believe backyard games with her dad, all the imaginary batters she'd faced. She thought about her last rotten pitch on the sidelines with Lonnie. She thought about Coach V in the dugout with the scorebook, pencil in hand, the blank squares in the inning, waiting to be filled in.

21. WILD IN A NEW WAY

*W*hile Molly was taking her warm-ups with Lonnie, the Sheridan team apparently noticed that the opposing pitcher was a girl. There was a mild commotion in the dugout. It wasn't as if they were a mile away. Molly could hear what they were saying plain as day. "Hey," she heard. "Check it out. On the mound. It's a girl."

Molly threw three fastballs and two knuckleballs, both only so-so, and the umpire brushed off the plate. From the Sheridan dugout came some halfhearted attempts at bench jockeying.

"How come you don't throw like a girl?"

"Hey, Baseball Barbie! What accessories do you come with?"

And then a man's stern voice. "That's enough. Knock it off."

Over the general din, Molly could distinctly hear Celia's hollering. Maybe because she was that loud, maybe because Molly was especially attuned to the pitch and frequency of her best friend's voice. "Show 'em what you got!" Celia was shouting. "You're the man, Molly! You're the man!"

The batter stepped in. Lonnie asked for a knuckleball and held up his mitt for a target. Molly started into her windup. She felt weirdly distant from herself. She felt robotic, as if she were on automatic pilot.

Halfway into her delivery, Molly realized that with runners on base, she should have been pitching from a stretch. Now it was too late to stop. She continued with her pitch, but the awareness of her mistake made her pause and jerk—it put a little hiccup in her windup. As a result, she held on to the ball too long and released it a split second too late. The pitch bounced at least two feet in front of the plate and skipped over Lonnie's shoulder to the backstop. The batter waved his arms to the runners, and each of them took another base while Lonnie retrieved the ball.

Runners on second and third now. Lonnie signaled for another floater. Molly nodded. This time she remembered to stretch properly. She brought her hands together at her waist, looked back at the runner leading off second base, and then directly at the kid on third. Neither of them was going anywhere.

This pitch was wild, too, just like the first, but wild in a new way. It was a real knuckler, no spin to it at all, but it came in high and inside. A lot of knucklers, most of them, dropped. But not this one. This one was a nonconformist.

155

This one just kept sailing—up, up, and away. The batter ducked out of the way, and once again Molly watched in mute, helpless horror while the ball went all the way to the backstop. Lonnie chased it, picked it up on the rebound, and turned toward the plate, arm cocked and ready to throw. But there was no one to throw to. The runner loped across the plate, and the Sheridan dugout exploded in cheers. The game was tied.

Lonnie walked slowly back to the plate, looking at Molly the whole time. She had forgotten to cover home, which was her responsibility. She was just standing there on the mound, gaping, a bystander. So much for smart baseball.

"Molly," Morales was saying. "Molly, Molly."

Was it possible that she had suffered some kind of baseball blackout? Molly had no clear recollection of the umpire calling time, no memory of Morales coming out of the dugout to join her on the mound. But here he was. Lonnie, too, breathing hard, a swatch of sweaty hair plastered across his forehead.

"You need to slow the game down a little," Morales said. "You're letting the game get away from you. You're acting like a passenger. You're letting the game happen to you. Do you know what I'm talking about?"

Molly nodded. She knew what he was talking about. She felt as if she'd been riding the game, like a roller coaster, hanging on, *barely* hanging on, feeling queasy, just hoping she could hold on until it stopped.

"It's your ball," Morales said. "You don't have to throw it until you're ready. It's okay to make them wait a little."

The umpire had positioned himself just a few yards away from them. He was eavesdropping, or maybe just trying to hurry them along. If so, Morales didn't seem to notice. He was slowing the game down himself.

"Do you think you can do that?" Morales asked.

Again Molly just nodded. She didn't trust her voice.

"I think you can, too," Morales said. "Don't forget to breathe."

Molly stood on the pitcher's rubber and tried to remember some Zen thing from her reading. *You must learn to wait properly*, the master told his student in the archery book. Lonnie had taken his position behind the plate. Molly decided just to look at the batter, really look at him. He was wearing a too-big batting helmet, and underneath it, he seemed to be grimacing. Trying to look fierce but, maybe, trying too hard. And he was standing awfully far from the plate. Maybe that last inside pitch had unsettled him a little.

Lonnie called for a fastball outside. He must have noticed the same thing she had. This kid wasn't eager to swing, and even if he did, he probably couldn't reach anything away.

"Go, McKinley!" some guy hollered from the sidelines. "Put 'em away!"

It was only a middle school game, but still, people were into it. This wasn't intramurals. It counted. That guy in the stands, whoever he was, he cared who won, and surprisingly, so did Molly. She really wanted to beat these guys. She wanted to win.

Molly stretched, paused, checked the runner. She paused again. It was her ball, Morales had told her. It's okay to make them wait a little. So she did. She waited. Molly heard Desmond shouting encouragement from left field. She heard Celia still hollering from the grandstand. She heard Mario Coppola at third base pounding his fist into his glove.

Molly rocked and threw. A nice pitch, straight and reasonably swift. It was on the outside half of the plate, thigh high. The batter watched it go by, and the umpire raised his right hand. "Strike one."

The Sheridan third-base coach starting clapping his hands. "That's the way, Pitch," he said. "Good effort." Molly took Lonnie's return throw.

Since when does a third-base coach offer happy talk to the opposing pitcher? Talk about patronizing! Molly glared in his direction. That slowed things down a little. He was a neat little man with rimless glasses and a clipboard. He'd probably read a whole shelf full of books about coaching baseball. He smiled at Molly. *Good effort? Good effort?* She stared a little longer, then spit.

Lonnie called for the same pitch, same spot. Molly stretched, checked the runners, and once again she took her sweet time doing it. She checked the jerky condescending coach, too, and then gave Lonnie a pitch right where he asked for it. He barely had to move his glove. The batter never moved. Strike two.

Molly enjoyed the satisfying *pop* the ball made in Lonnie's mitt and the little puff of dust that wafted from it. It was a pressure situation and all that, but that little puff of dust just seemed beautiful all by itself. It was something that even Coach V, as meticulous a scorekeeper as he was, had no symbol for. You'd have to write a poem about it, a haiku maybe. It would never appear in the official book, but it was real.

Lonnie stood to return the ball. "One more!" he shouted. "Just one more is all we need!" It was something to see him so pumped up. This was a new side of him.

This time he called for the knuckler, and Molly nodded. Again, at the stretch, she paused, breathed, and just let in the sounds of the game. Molly heard the third-base coach clapping his hands. She heard a siren in the distance. And she heard a new voice from the grandstand, a familiar voice, so familiar she couldn't place it right away. This voice wasn't shouting instructions. It was just saying her name, "Molly, Molly." This voice wasn't excited or urgent. It sounded calm and loving.

Molly released this knuckleball and watched with something like curiosity. Right out of her hand, it felt good. It came in a little high and perfectly spinless. It seemed to be vibrating. Then it did what looked like a double dip and dropped into Lonnie's glove. The batter took a halfhearted swat at it, but he was way off, not even close.

Lonnie held the ball up to the umpire to show that he'd snared it. He took off his mask. He had a huge grin on his face.

The umpire raised his arm. The inning was over.

Molly had situated herself in the corner of the dugout, where she figured she ought to contemplate her generally dismal performance alone. She'd thrown two wild pitches and let in the tying run. It was the sort of outing that caused big league pitchers to kick water coolers and pout. She was supposed to sit in solitude and meditate on her failure, consider its weight and color, what it looked like in Coach V's scorebook. She was supposed to stew about it for a while. In baseball, if you didn't hang your head after a failure, people thought you didn't care.

The thing was, even though she knew she was supposed to feel downhearted, Molly, truth be told, didn't really feel all that glum. For one thing, her teammates wouldn't leave her alone. It was hard to wallow in self-loathing when people kept talking to her. "That was some pitch, Williams," Ben Malone told her. "That kid looked *paralyzed*." Eli Krause walked past and turned her hat around. Everett Sheets handed her a cup of water he'd drawn for her from the cooler. "Don't worry about a shaky start," he said. "You found your groove." The parade of consolation and support reminded her a little of her dad's wake and funeral, that long endless line. Somehow, though, this was better. Somehow, these clichés really did cheer her up. They made her feel like one of the guys.

But the real reason she was feeling anything but glum was simple: the voice. As she was coming off the field after the third out, looking up into the stands as she jogged toward the dugout, it hit her. She realized whose voice it was. Someone whose face she was never going to find in the grandstand.

It must have been some kind of hallucination, brought on, probably, by stress. The sound of her father's voice saying her name. But even if it was a mistake, some kind of biochemical brain event, she felt better. She heard what she heard, and she felt transformed, energized. She felt as if she'd been given some kind of injection—a shot of her dad. All of a sudden a couple of wild pitches didn't seem quite so tragic.

On the field, Desmond Davis had doubled to right field and then stolen third. He was the go-ahead run. Lloyd Coleman struck out, but with Mario Coppola at bat, Coach Morales signaled for the suicide squeeze play. Mario put down a perfect bunt, and Desmond thundered across the plate.

Molly whooped and hollered along with everyone else and stood with the mob of her teammates and pounded Desmond when he got to the dugout. Molly was happy for him and happy for the team. She also felt tremendously relieved. This was no longer the game she'd lost. She was off the hook.

"Williams on deck," Coach V shouted over the top of their happy noise. "Vogel in the hole." It hadn't occurred to Molly that she might be called upon to hit. She grabbed a helmet and found her favorite bat and stepped out of the dugout to loosen up.

Everett Sheets was at bat. He was digging himself in, kicking the dirt with his cleats, getting settled, slowing the game down in his own fashion.

Molly took a swing of the bat and on her follow-through sneaked a peek into the stands. It wasn't professional, but she couldn't help herself. What Molly saw tugged at her heart a little. All the moms and dads, shoulder to shoulder, kids from school, little brothers and sisters scrunched together—Celia right in the middle of the crowd, her head bent over her lap in concentration, stitching like mad. Beyond the grandstands were a few solitary onlookers, keeping their distance. One was a pacing man, too nervous apparently to sit still, Everett Sheets's dad, probably—they had the same curly hair. There were even a couple of dogs, one chewing a tennis ball, another getting its belly scratched by a little girl. All together, the scene could have been a Norman Rockwell painting. It would be called *Loved Ones*, which was a corny phrase Molly had heard a million times and never really thought about one way or another. Now, for the first time, she didn't just understand it, she *felt* it.

The umpire called a strike on Everett, and while he returned to his excavations in the batter's box, Molly took another swing and stole another glance at the crowd.

This time she saw her. Standing off a few paces from the grandstand, all by herself, a solitary figure. Her mother. She must have come right from work. She must have cut out early, which she never did.

Her mom was wearing a navy skirt and jacket, a white blouse, heels. On her lapel there was a pin Molly had made for her years ago as a Mother's Day gift, glue and colored beads, homely but sincere. Back then Molly still believed her mother when she said homemade was best.

To see her here was almost as unlikely, almost as shocking, as it had been to hear her father's voice. Her mother at a baseball game! Another miracle.

When she saw Molly, she gave a wave. It was quick and shy, a mini wave. If you'd blinked, you might have missed it.

Molly wanted to acknowledge her, but she didn't want to be unprofessional about it. She touched the brim of her batting helmet, which seemed like a baseball thing to do. It was her own private baseball sign. It meant "Hi, Mom." It meant "I'm glad you're here."

Her mother seemed to get it. She raised her hand and touched the brim of her hat, which she wasn't wearing, so it was a kind of comical gesture—her hand in the air, touching nothing. But Molly understood. It was the thought that counted.

Everett, meanwhile, had grounded out for the third out. Molly returned to the dugout, took off her helmet, and watched her teammates grab their gloves and prepare to take the field for the bottom of the seventh, the last half inning.

"Molly?" It was Morales, standing behind her, watching her watch her teammates take the field.

"Coach?"

"Care to join them?" He was smiling, almost.

"On the mound?" Molly had just assumed that he'd seen enough, that she was done for the day.

"Yes, Molly," he said. "The mound." He pointed. "That bump? It's that big circle of dirt in the middle of the field."

In the last inning Molly didn't hear the voice—she heard her teammates, and Coach Morales, calling out singsong encouragement; she heard Celia hollering and whistling from the stands; she could hear Lonnie humming from behind the plate; she just didn't hear *that* voice. But she didn't need to.

On the mound Molly felt like she was humming. She felt entirely at ease, somehow. She felt as if she were wearing her dad's old beat-up magic hat. As if no harm could come to her now.

The third-base coach was clapping his hands, trying to rally his team, sounding just a little bit desperate now, but Molly wasn't really tuned in to him. She was throwing to Lonnie's glove, playing catch, the same game of catch she'd started so many years ago. Her butterfly had once again become full of mischief. It performed a couple of tricks even Molly had never seen before, a couple of new dips and dives. It was like a kid showing off. *Look at me!* it seemed to be saying. *Look what I can do!*

The first batter tapped a ball out in front of the plate, where Lonnie pounced on it and threw him out. The next batter was Mr. Mustache. He swung helplessly at three knucklers and sat down.

One more out and the game would be over. The next hitter sent a hard ground ball to Lloyd Coleman at shortstop, who fielded it cleanly and then promptly threw it about ten feet over Everett's head at first base.

The runner advanced to second base, and the ball was thrown back to Molly. She noticed that Lloyd had returned to his position at shortstop, but he didn't look right. His chest was heaving. She could hear him breathing in shrill, whistling gasps, like a teapot ready to boil.

Now, upset about making an error, he didn't look like a tough guy. He didn't look like a wannabe thug, he didn't look like the kid who'd so intimidated her. He was just a boy trying not to cry.

Molly did what a good teammate should do. She took a few steps toward Lloyd. Kneeled down and pretended to tie her shoe. Gave him time to compose himself. "Shake it off," she said. "We'll get the next guy. No problem."

Lloyd tugged at his cap. "Sorry," he said. "My fault."

"Forget about it," Molly said. "It's nothing. NBD."

"Right," he said.

Molly stood up. *You made an error!* She felt like saying. *A bad throw. So what? It's a baseball game. A game. Who really cares? A bad throw? In the great scheme of things? A bad throw?* Of course she didn't say that. She understood that your own errors always feel tragic.

Molly took a couple more steps toward Lloyd, and he met her halfway. She held her glove over her mouth the way big league players did when they conferred on the field. Molly figured that they didn't want their opponents to read their lips, but the sight of two men talking through gloves, their faces covered with them, like jet pilots wearing oxygen masks, always amused her. It seemed like such a guy thing.

"My glove smells awful," Molly said. "How 'bout yours?"

Lloyd's face relaxed. He looked so relieved, so grateful. What had she given him, really? Not much. How hard was it? Not hard at all. It was easy.

Lloyd covered his face with his own glove then. "Terrible," he said. Something like a laugh came out from behind the glove. "It smells terrible. Like mink oil and sweat."

Out of the corner of her eye, Molly glimpsed the umpire coming out to get them moving. "I suppose I should pitch the ball," she said.

"I suppose," Lloyd said. He still had his glove over his

face, but Molly could see that his eyes were happy now. He was ready.

The next batter was a stout, serious-looking boy, biting his lip, squeezing the bat—his whole body was a clenched fist. Molly almost felt sorry for him. Almost. She struck him out on three pitches.

22. YES CRAZY

"Joan of Arc heard voices," Celia said. "She was a saint."

"So did Charles Manson," Molly said. "He was a psycho."

They were sitting together on Molly's front steps. It was getting dark. There were clouds rolling in, and it was starting to smell like rain.

"You think I'm crazy?" Molly asked. They'd been talking over the game and had covered almost every angle, rehashed just about every aspect, on and off the field, chopped it thoroughly to pieces—Molly's performance, her mother's surprising appearance, the fact that Lonnie looked good in his gear.

Molly had finally told Celia about what she'd heard.

The voice. She knew it was going to sound crazy when she explained it, and it did. But it was not the sort of thing she could keep to herself. Molly had to tell someone, and Celia was her someone.

"Yes," Celia said.

"Yes?" Molly said. "Yes crazy?"

"Yes crazy," Celia said. "Absolutely crazy."

"You think so?" Molly said.

"But good crazy," Celia said.

"Right," Molly said. "Because I've always thought of insanity as a big plus."

"You know what I mean," Celia said. "You're not ordinary. You like to act that way, but you're not. You know how to pretend. You can pass. But you can't fool me. You have a gift. You've been touched. Whatever you want to call it. You have a magic pitch. That's a gift. And you heard your dad today. He was sending you a message. That's another gift."

Molly thought of the word "gifted." Sometimes teachers had called her that. Before Honors, she was in the program for the gifted and talented. Molly had always thought "gifted" was just another word for "smart," but now she understood what it really meant. She said it out loud, "I'm gifted," and Celia didn't laugh at her.

"You *are*," Celia said, so forcefully it was startling. "You *are* gifted."

They sat together then for a while, neither of them saying anything. It was a good silence. Celia took her stitching project out of a bag and fiddled with that. Molly watched some bats flitting low in the sky, swooping and diving. She listened to the sounds on the street, a dog barking, which she knew was Hank, the gray-faced boxer from down the block, the wind rustling the leaves of the trees overhead.

It was her street, her neighborhood, her life. She knew that someday in the future it would not be hers anymore. But she would remember it, she would treasure it, she would miss it. She would hold it in her heart. She knew that someday she would look back at this very moment and miss it. "Remember that night," she could hear herself telling Celia years from now. "Remember how we sat on the steps. . . ." She felt like crying. Never had life seemed more beautiful and more sad. Talk about crazy!

Molly heard something then, a rattling and clicking. She looked down the block. There was something coming down the street toward them, a shadow in motion. It was Lonnie on his old blue bike. He turned up the driveway, rode a few feet across the lawn, and dismounted on the fly, letting his bike drop on the grass.

"Molly," Lonnie said, a little breathlessly. He was wearing a T-shirt and a baggy pair of cargo shorts. His hair looked damp, fresh from the shower. He arrived with such Paul Revere urgency, she expected some big, important news.

Molly hadn't seen him since the general riot of celebration and congratulation on the field after the game. Before she'd been able to get in a word with him, alone, he'd disappeared into the school and the boys' locker room. She wanted to thank him for being so solid behind the plate.

"Hey, Lonnie," Celia said, and he seemed to notice just then that she was there, too.

"Oh," Lonnie said. "Hey, Celia." And he turned back toward Molly.

"I've got something for you," Lonnie said.

"The boy comes bearing gifts," Celia said. "I knew I liked him."

Lonnie reached into one of his big pockets and pulled out—a baseball.

"It's a ball," Celia said.

"It's the *game* ball," Lonnie said. "I stuffed it in my pocket after the last out. Nobody asked for it back."

"It's a stolen ball," Celia said.

"It's like a keepsake," Molly explained. "A souvenir."

"Wow," Celia said. "This is like some kind of ancient ritual. Some Romeo and Juliet, Shakespeare thing. Are you pledging your troth?"

"My troth?" Lonnie said. He looked a little scared.

"Knock it off," Molly said. She took the ball from Lonnie. "Thank you," she said. It was scuffed and stained with grass and dirt, which Molly liked—that old-school look. The ball felt good in her hand. Her time on the mound that day was already starting to seem distant, even dreamlike. This would remind her it had been real. If it weren't so late, if it weren't already almost dark, she would have asked Lonnie if he wanted to play some catch. She wouldn't mind throwing a little. More craziness.

"Would you care to join us?" Celia said. While Molly had been daydreaming, Lonnie had been standing there, awkwardly and expectantly, as if he were waiting for a tip or something.

"May I?" asked Lonnie, gone all formal suddenly. He was wary of Celia, Molly thought—she had that effect on people.

"Yes, please," Molly said. "Pull up a piece of step."

They sat there, the three of them, Lonnie on Molly's left, Celia on her right. Lonnie noticed Celia's project. "What is that?" he wanted to know.

"Good question," Celia said. "Time will tell."

Lonnie had more questions for Celia, real questions. He wanted to know all about what she was doing, how she was doing it. Before long Celia was giving him a lesson, Stitching 101, and he was a pretty quick study.

"Do you know how many stitches there are in a baseball?" Molly asked. It was something she knew. It was the sort of thing an announcer would tell you during a slow point in a game. It was baseball trivia. She must have filed the information away, and now she blurted it out. "A hundred and eight."

"You know, Lonnie," Celia said, "you could probably make your own baseballs. Cut some fabric, stuff 'em, and stitch 'em up."

"I suppose," Lonnie said.

"Not to play with," Celia said. "They'd be works of art."

Celia was riffing now, Molly was pretty sure, just messing around the way she did, but Lonnie looked interested.

"It would be the coolest modern art ever," Celia said. "The Albright-Knox would be all over it. You could do for baseballs what Andy Warhol did for soup."

"Hmmm," Lonnie said. Molly could see the wheels turning.

"You could experiment with different textures, different colors," Celia said. "You could paint little landscapes on them."

Molly tried to imagine what it would be like to throw a

painted baseball. It might be fun. It would freak out the batter for sure.

"You could do some abstract expressionist thing," Celia said. "Use different-colored rectangles, maybe, like those paintings we studied by what's-his-name."

"Mondrian." Lonnie knew. Was Celia serious? Was Lonnie going to start making baseball art? Molly had no idea. There was no way to predict. What a couple of interesting friends she had.

It started to rain then, just a few irregular, fat drops at first, then more steadily. Under cover of the roof, Molly felt safe and protected. When she was little, she used to sit here and watch thunderstorms. She could see the sheets of rain pounding the streets, sometimes even feel a mist, but not get soaked.

"Your bike," Molly said.

"That's okay," Lonnie said. So they sat there, the three of them, not talking, just watching the world get wet.

The door swung open behind them. Molly's mother was standing there with something in her hand. It was dark now. The rain had passed. Molly had been thinking about getting up, about standing and stretching her legs. She had even announced her intention to do just that. She just hadn't gotten around to it.

Celia stood immediately. "Mrs. Williams," she said. "It's a pleasure to see you."

Celia had this way with adults. She shifted into a style that was excessively polite, almost. She would be formal, so formal it was clear that it was a kind of game, one that parents could play, too. She managed to be respectful and playful both—smart, but not a smart aleck. Not many kids could pull it off, but Celia could.

Molly's mom smiled. "It's a pleasure to see *you*, Celia," she said. "It always is." Molly could see that what her mother was holding was a tray with some tall glasses on it.

"I like what you've done with your hair," Celia said. "It's very becoming."

"Thank you," her mother said.

"I believe you know Lonnie," Celia said, and gestured in his direction. He stood up, sort of, in a kind of awkward crouch.

"Hello, Lonnie."

"Hi," he said.

"I was thinking you might be getting thirsty," Molly's mother said. "Would you care for some lemonade?"

Lemonade? Lemonade? *If life gives you lemons, make lemonade.* Molly had heard that plenty of times. Probably it was something her dad had said. But Molly doubted there was a single lemon in their kitchen. Where did her mother come up with lemonade? Molly didn't know about any frozen or powdered lemonade in the house either, nothing in a can or a carton. Her mother wasn't even the lemonade type. And yet there it was, big as life, three tall glasses, complete with straws and clinking ice.

So Molly had to admit, to herself anyway, that her mother could be something of a dark horse. Molly might have underestimated her a little. Her mother could still surprise. She knew how to mix things up. She apparently could throw a trick pitch or two of her own.

"We'd love some lemonade," Celia said. "Wouldn't we, kids?"

Molly's mother handed around the glasses, which they accepted. They thanked her. Molly took a sip. Maybe it was a mix, but it tasted real.

"Would you care to join us?" Celia said to Molly's mother. "There's plenty of room." She pointed grandly to the step, as if she were inviting her to be seated on some fancy velvet-covered chair and not on a slab of concrete.

"We're basking in the glow of today's triumph," Celia said. "We're savoring it."

They moved together to make room, and Molly's mother took a seat next to Celia. Molly hoped her mother wouldn't start to interrogate Lonnie, and to her credit, she didn't. She seemed to fall into their mood of quiet contemplation. They sat there together in silence and looked at the street. It seemed to Molly like another haiku moment. *Rain on the sidewalk / On the steps with your mother / Lemon on your tongue*. But she wasn't about to spoil it with words.

Molly nudged Lonnie's foot with hers, gently, secretly, and he nudged her right back. Celia stitched. Her mother stretched out her legs. For once, she wasn't doing anything, not accomplishing anything at all.

To be with her mom, and Celia, and Lonnie, like this, all of them together, it felt a little embarrassing to Molly. It felt more than a little odd. But it also felt good. In a weird way. This was not literally her family, not in the strict sense—not biologically, not technically. But as they sat squeezed together, as Molly's and Lonnie's knees touched, as they sipped their lemonade and thought their own thoughts, Molly felt connected and safe. You didn't have to lock arms to make a human chain.

Maybe it wasn't a real family. But it was good enough.

23. MOONLIGHT

*I*t was after midnight. Molly was standing alone in her backyard. The rain had stopped, and the clouds had blown away. There was a nearly full moon in the sky—just a sliver missing—shining down on her. Tonight, in the Rybaks' house next door, there was no television glowing. The red light of her radio tower was blinking in the distance.

A couple of hours earlier Molly had said goodbye finally, first to Celia and then to Lonnie. Lonnie had given her a quick kiss, a little awkward and off center, but it seemed like a good start. Before going up to bed, Molly had said good night to her mom and had tried her best to thank her. "For . . . ," Molly said. "You know."

"I know," her mother had said, and Molly believed she

did. "And you can stop thinking about moving," her mother told her. "Is that okay?" Molly didn't have to say anything. Her mother knew it was okay, more than okay.

It wasn't that Molly couldn't sleep. She wasn't restless, she hadn't been tossing and turning. It was more like she didn't want to sleep. She wasn't quite ready for the day to end. She'd debriefed with Celia; now she wanted to debrief herself.

Moonlight, people used to believe, made you crazy. Molly had read that somewhere, or maybe her dad told her. "Lunar" had to do with the moon; a "lunatic" was a crazy person. She was a girl standing barefoot under the moon in the middle of the night in the wet grass of her backyard with a baseball in her hand. *She* was a lunatic!

Tomorrow might be a different story, but right at that moment, Molly felt that Celia was right. She was crazy, good crazy. She was gifted. She was touched. No doubt, probably soon, she would freeze up on the mound, her knuckleball would once again refuse to knuckle. She'd feud some more with her mother. She'd probably get impatient with Lonnie, suffer some new indignity from Lloyd Coleman. She was light-years away from closure.

She would always miss her dad. Always. That wasn't ever going to go away. That had been an amputation. That limb was never going to grow back. It would always ache.

Once, with her dad, late at night, she'd watched an old black-and-white baseball movie about a pitcher who'd lost a leg in a hunting accident. Outfitted with a wooden leg, cheered on by a loyal wife, he returned to pitch in the majors. The movie was sappy and heartwarming, all about old-fashioned grit and courage. It was supposed to be inspirational. She was just a kid, but Molly could tell that the Hollywood version left a lot out. They never showed what was left of his leg, for one thing, the stump.

What Molly remembered best was the herky-jerky way this pitcher threw on his new leg. He was so stiff and awkward it was almost painful to watch, but somehow he got batters out. It wasn't pretty, but he got it done. Not that anyone would choose to lose a leg, but Molly couldn't help but wonder if this guy's new wooden-legged windup might have been some sort of advantage. His motion was odd and unpredictable, so unlike any other, it must have thrown batters off.

Molly knew now that even though she'd lost her dad, she could still, just like the one-legged pitcher in the movie, find a way, in her own fashion, in her own peculiar style, to get up, get to the mound, throw strikes. She was no Hollywood hero. Whatever grit was, she didn't think she had very much. But she could do what needed to be done.

Molly held the scuffed game ball in her hand. It felt right. Reassuringly solid. Her arm felt loose. She found her spot in the yard. She peered in for a sign. A knuckler? The butterfly? She nodded.

She could almost see him there, squatting in the moonlight, giving her a target. Her dad. Who knew so much about baseball and grammar, who late one night on a dark road had committed one terrible error, who, one time, even though she'd needed him, had dozed off, lost control. How could she not forgive him?

Molly went into her motion. She pumped her arms, she rocked, she pivoted. She brought her arm back and then forward, hard, over the top. She let go.